BOOKS BY QUINN AVERY
www.QuinnAvery.com

BEXLEY SQUIRES MYSTERY SERIES

*The Dead Girl's Stilettos*

*The Million Dollar Collar*

*The Guard's Last Watch*

*The Skeleton Key's Secrets*

*The Notebook's Hidden Truths*

*The Neighbor's Dark Past*

STANDALONE ROMANTIC SUSPENSE/THRILLERS

*What They Never Said*

*In Her Father's Shadow*

*Woman Over the Edge*

*Deadly Paradise*

*Lost Girls of Kato*

*Moscow Mules & Murder*

*Right Across the Bay*

**CHILDREN'S BOOKS WRITTEN BY QUINN**

*Dogs Don't Have Fins*

*Dogs Don't Have Antlers*

*The Dead Girl's Stilettos*
*The Million Dollar Collar*
*The Guard's Last Watch*
*The Skeleton Key's Secrets*
*The Notebook's Hidden Truths*
*The Neighbor's Dark Past*

# THE
# SKELETON KEY'S SECRETS

A BEXLEY SQUIRES MYSTERY

## QUINN AVERY

The Skeleton Key's Secrets: A Bexley Squires Mystery



Cover: Najla Qamber Designs

Photograph: Jen Naumann Photography

Model: Brooke Stindtman

www.QuinnAvery.com

# PROLOGUE

## PAPAYA SPRINGS, CALIFORNIA

### DECEMBER 27TH

Retired U.S. Navy Captain Dominic Ferguson observed his daughters interacting with their boyfriends from across the steak house's wide table, feeling a misplaced sense of pride. He acknowledged that he had very little to do with the girls' upbringing, and he wasn't going to take the credit from his late wife. Eloise had been a saint for putting up with his behaviors, essentially single-parenting their daughters until cancer took her from them. Still, he wondered if he'd had a hand in the girls' choice of romantic interests as both men were former military and imperfect in their actions, just like himself.

Both Cineste and Bexley had been through their share of unpleasantness as well. But ever since his oldest had moved back to the area, they'd each become focused on their futures. Cineste, his youngest, had enrolled back into college after dropping out during a party stage, and was planning to become a social worker. Bexley had put her education in journalism to good use, working on becoming the area's go-to private detective after inheriting an established agency from her employer. In Dominic's eyes, neither profession was exactly noble, but they were still leaps and bounds ahead of their recently discovered half-sister.

The weight of his past mistakes caused Dominic to slump against the padded chair. A queue of endless women had produced at least one illegitimate child—that he'd been informed of anyway— and both Bexley and Cineste had refused to accept the existence of another sibling. In fact, when he first introduced Sadie to the girls, Bexley had taken off and refused to meet with him again until recently. Although Cineste had somehow convinced Bexley to come to their family Christmas dinner, his oldest had been cold throughout the entire meal, and refused to make eye contact.

The extramarital affairs were only the tip of the

iceberg when it came to his list of regrets. Fortunately, he'd done everything within his power to keep his other secrets hidden from his daughters. From what he could tell, they were oblivious.

He was beyond ready to turn what was left of his life around. Once he'd retired, he'd decided it was time to focus his energy on the things that mattered. His three girls were now his number one priority. And that meant making sure they were living their best lives. Since he hadn't properly cared for any of them in their formative years, he was going to make damn sure they were set with good men who could provide for them and his future grandchildren.

Cineste wasn't afraid of being affectionate in front of her father. More often than not, she was cozied up to her boyfriend, practically sitting in the young man's lap, and would kiss him every couple of minutes. Alex, on the other hand, seemed mindful of Dominic's presence, and kept his hands to himself. Although Alex hadn't made it through SEAL training, he'd recently enrolled in construction management classes with a community college, and held down a good job with a well-respected contractor.

Dominic warily eyed the heavily tattooed,

former Coast Guardsman sitting beside Bexley. After thirty-six years in the military, Dominic had never given into the craze that'd become increasingly popular in the Navy. Although Brewer had also been polite and respectful throughout the evening, Dominic suspected anyone who had spent that much time and money in a tattoo parlor was out to prove something to the world. He found it curious that Bexley treated Brewer as if he was an old friend, while Dominic caught Brewer giving his eldest the kind of looks a man gives a woman when he's ready to settle down and give her babies.

Leaning forward, Dominic steepled his fingers underneath his chin. "Tell me again, Brewer…what is it you do for a living?"

Amidst a laugh in response to something Brewer said, Bexley's shoulders stiffened. Her eyes slowly shifted upward to meet Dominic's. "I already told you, he owns and manages Hawkins Auto Body."

Dominic abhorred the way hatred rippled off his eldest, although maybe he deserved it. Regardless, it was an issue he planned to address another time when they were alone. "Is it profitable? Is that what you plan on doing until retirement?"

Bexley's eyebrows darted down and her lips parted. Brewer quickly shot her a sharp look that made her think twice. *Good for him,* Dominic thought.

Then Brewer cleared his throat and raised his chin. "Actually, sir, I've been thinking a degree in mechanical engineering may be a viable option somewhere down the road."

"He doesn't need to know that," Bexley snapped at him. "What you're already doing is a perfectly respectable profession."

With a wry smirk, Brewer whispered something in her ear. Bexley promptly crossed her arms, and turned her angry expression on Dominic. "Everyone at this table knows whatever we choose to do with our lives won't be enough for you, so you can spare us the lecture you were planning on giving Brewer about preparing for his future." Then she stood, addressing her little sister. "I can't take any more of this. We're leaving."

"Bexley, wait," Dominic said, willing himself to remain calm. "Will there ever come a time when you can say goodbye in a civilized manner?"

Before turning away, his eldest answered with an angry glare that Dominic felt in the depths of his gut. He suspected Bexley would never forgive him.

DOMINIC BEGGED FOR THE RELIEF OF SLEEP TO erase his dark thoughts. He remained troubled by the family dinner as Bexley made it clear she wanted nothing to do with her father. She despised him, and he didn't know how to make things right. What if it was too late for them to make amends?

Around two in the morning, Dominic received a disturbing call. After packing an overnight bag, he found a way to head north.

On a quiet highway a handful of miles past Sacramento, he was overwhelmed with the need to sleep. He stopped at a gas station on the far end of a small town to grab the biggest cup of coffee available.

The middle-aged gas station attendant was the last person to see Dominic Ferguson alive.

# PART I

# CHAPTER ONE

## LOS ANGELES, CALIFORNIA

DECEMBER 28TH

Bexley Squires awoke to the quiet ding of her cell phone. She'd become an exceptionally light sleeper since taking over the reins of Stronghold Investigations. The ins and outs of the business were always on her mind as she was afraid of somehow destroying J.J.'s legacy. Although her mentor made it clear that he was always available for anything she needed, he was on oxygen because of his recently diagnosed lung disease. She hated to bother him with little details.

She was first confused by daylight peeking through an unfamiliar set of windows until she remembered she'd finally taken Brewer Hawkins up on his open-ended offer to spend the night. Although he had the means to afford a serious upgrade from the motel room on the south side of L.A., memories of his murdered fiancée and their unborn child in the last place he called home were still too difficult for him to move on.

Surprisingly, Bexley caught more than a handful of hours of sleep in what felt like ages. She wondered if it had something to do with the comfort that came with Brewer's presence, or even the scent of leather and masculinity that lingered even though he must've left while she was asleep. He had a way of soothing Bexley without having to do or say anything out of the ordinary. Sometimes it scared her just how much she liked having him around. She was even more terrified by how much it would hurt when he left.

Swiping her phone off the nightstand, she yawned as her foggy gaze scrolled over a text from her former defense attorney-turned-friend Luke Jacobs.

*Turn on the local news*

She bolted upright, folding her bare legs beneath her as she pointed the remote at the motel's outdated TV, scrolling to the Papaya Springs affiliate channel.

She caught the tail end of something about the president visiting another country for peace talks. Then there was a transition from the studio to where WCSO's lead anchor, Kelsi Thomas, stood outside the Currie County Courthouse in a dark trench coat, curly red hair tucked beneath a beanie cap.

"Three months after Papaya Springs' former Mayor Edward Hoffman and former District Attorney Karl Jenkins were arrested in connection to suspected drug smuggling—among other serious felonies including attempted murder and murder in the first degree—the pair have allegedly entered plea bargains. The details of their pleas have not yet been made public, but they're expected to appear in court later this week. The pair's defense attorneys and DA Mariah Holmes were unavailable for comment."

As Kelsi continued to summarize the men's situation, a numb sensation filled Bexley from head to toe. They replayed the video from the duo's first appearance in court. The clip included a brief shot of her sitting in the gallery between Luke and Brewer. Her ex-boyfriend, Detective

Grayson Rivers, watched on from the back of the room.

Unease still thrummed through Bexley with memories of bringing the Mayor and DA to justice, followed by the suicide of Lieutenant Baker. She still questioned whether or not she acted in haste, and if things would've ended differently if she'd called for backup. Grayson and the lieutenant's family seemed to think she was directly responsible for his fate.

With the sound of a key jiggling in the door lock, she clicked the TV off. Brewer stepped inside with a cup of coffee and a garment bag draped over his arm. His captivatingly handsome face twisted with a grin and a raised eyebrow. "A guy could get used to this sight every morning."

Something about the man's confident demeanor never failed to make Bexley secretly swoon like a teenager. That paired with his extensive tattoo collection, the way he tucked his chin-length brown hair behind his ears, and his meticulously groomed facial hair made for a delectable package.

He haphazardly tossed the bag on the chair by the window and joined Bexley, handing her the steaming cup while bending for a lingering kiss. Her lips tingled wildly as if it were the first time and not the hundredth—or however many blissful times they'd spent getting lost in each other. *God, she'd miss that mouth.*

He drew away, his warm brown eyes dilated. "My shirt looks good on you—I wouldn't be sad if you wore it every night."

Humming, she tugged on the neckline of the white T-shirt he wore with his favorite pair of blue jeans, faded from constant wear. "You might change your mind when you realize it's the last clean thing you own."

"The new maid quit doing my laundry." He laid down on his back at her side, tucking an arm behind his head. "She seems to think Big Dick would fire her if he found out I was paying her for side jobs."

"Side jobs…plural? Do I want to know what else this new maid is doing under your employ?" Bexley lowered to her side, sipping on her favorite brew while admiring his strong features. There was a faint scar embedded among the thick hairs of his left eyebrow that she hadn't noticed until they'd started to become intimate, and it made him even more enduring. He'd been through hell and back, and came out a better man. Her eyes rounded. "Hold on. Is this new maid cute?"

His eyes twinkled with amusement. "Is that jealousy I hear, Squires?"

"I'm merely trying to picture what type of woman could possibly be immune to the charms of Brewer Hawkins."

"She's ancient…like eighty," he deadpanned. "Smells like mothballs…giant moles everywhere." He draped an arm over Bexley's hip, dragging her close enough to kiss the side of her head. "She's totally atrocious."

Breathing in his tobacco-laced scent, she was grateful he'd made a point not to smoke around her since J.J.'s diagnosis. Though she doubted she could convince Brewer to quit altogether, she appreciated the thoughtful gesture.

She playfully poked him in the side. "If you're done smoking in here, you should give the room a new paint job to get rid of the lingering smell. A little whitewash treatment would do wonders. You could even install one of those rolling barn doors between the bed and armchair to make a second room…add a little character."

He chuckled. "Here I thought you already loved me for my character—untraditional and a little rough around the edges."

She mentally winced with the term of endearment, even if he was being flippant. "A little rough?" she teased. "Buddy, you were sculpted with a chainsaw."

Grinning back at her, he shrugged and sat up. "Maybe I'll be ready to live somewhere else after I'm done serving my time."

Bexley's heart strings tugged with the mention of his impending fate. After he'd recently taken a plea bargain, admitting to being an accessory to drug smuggling after he'd left the Coast Guard, the judge had ordered a pre-sentence investigation. Brewer's final hearing had yet to be scheduled, and it was causing Bexley more anxiety than she could handle. Their relationship had become comfortable, without any pressure. She wasn't ready for the dramatic changes she'd be forced to face once he was sent away.

Desperate for a change of subject, she rolled up beside him and jerked her head toward the garment bag. Interestingly enough, it sported the logo of her best friend's favorite department store. "You've only been around Kiersten for a handful of weeks, and you're already taking on her bad habits. Next thing I know you'll be attending fashion week together."

"I asked her to help me with a little surprise." He grinned in a sheepish way that reminded her of the seventeen-year-old boy who'd been one of their school's outcasts. "You're getting dressed up tonight, Squires. We're going out."

She motioned to the T-shirt hanging off one of her shoulders. "I thought you said I looked good in this."

His grin grew as a mischievous look sparked in his eyes. "Believe me, I'd be all for you wearing that. But where we're going, you might feel a little uncomfortable."

"A proper night out on the town?" She titled her head. "Since when did you decide it takes more than impressive muscles and a fast motorcycle to woo a girl?"

"When I remembered our high school reunion's tonight."

All her excitement went out the window. "And you're suggesting we go?" She'd recently deleted the reunion from her phone's calendar, laughing at herself for bothering to mark it down in the first place. With a shake of her head, she snorted. "Did you have a lobotomy for breakfast?"

He chuckled. "Come on, Squires…it'll be fun. Kiersten and Luke will be there. You can dance to a little Spice Girls, have some umbrella drinks with old friends, reminisce about the days when I cheated off your tests." Laughing a little harder, he weaved his fingers through her hair and lightly tugged. "What do you say? Let's stir some shit up in this town...give those rich pricks something to talk about. Besides, I promised Kiersten I'd talk you into going."

She was surprised by his insistence, considering he'd been a loner and abandoned their senior year to enlist because of an abusive foster parent. And she wasn't exactly excited by the idea of seeing Grayson again. Once she made it clear there was no chance of getting back together, he'd become bitter. She personally hadn't received an invite to the reunion because Grayson's ex-wife was in charge.

On the other hand, Brewer had been sweet enough to arrange for Kiersten to set her up for the night. And a part of her kind of dug the idea of making her former classmates jealous once they saw Brewer's transformation.

Meeting his hopeful expression, she blew out a long, exaggerated breath while popping to her feet. "I'll do whatever it takes to get you to stop giving me that baby Yoda face. Seriously, Hawk, have some pride." As she started for the bathroom, she realized she'd been spending way too much time with her Star Wars obsessed assistant. Maybe a night of socializing with the outside world would do her good.

---

THE PARTY WAS ALREADY IN FULL SWING BY THE TIME they entered the ballroom inside the Papaya Springs Royal posh hotel. Hundreds of Bexley's classmates and their significant others formed clusters throughout the room, the din of their conversation and laughter almost equal decibels to the old school rock blasting from a wall of speakers surrounding a deejay. Pretentiousness stunk up the grand room like an Uber driver's air freshener.

Bexley didn't realize she'd frozen in the doorway, gaze fixed on the same group of people she swore she'd never see again, until Brewer tugged on her hand. "No changing your mind on me now, B. The way you look in that? I'm planning to parade you around all night—show the other guys what they missed out on."

When her cheeks warmed, she glanced down at the ensemble handpicked by Kiersten. The white, one-shouldered pantsuit with a wide sash around her waist was more comfortable than any dress she'd worn, and it fit her personality. The heeled sandals had taken a little adjustment, but she adored the chandelier earrings in her favorite shade of cobalt blue. The excessive hours she'd spent on the back of Brewer's motorcycle had tanned her skin, giving her an unexpected glow that was accentuated by the flattering outfit. And in addition to running along the beach with Brewer nearly every morning before work, they'd begun lifting weights together. Finally, thanks to Kiersten's guidance, Bexley had done a decent job of curling her shoulder-length hair in subtle waves. Next to Brewer's slim-fitting white button-down and light blue jeans, they made a striking pair.

"Smile for the camera!" a woman called out in a nasally pitch.

Bexley glanced up right as a bright flash flooded them. The blonde lowered her bejeweled smart phone, scowling. Grayson's ex-wife, Amanda Classon, was nearly unrecognizable. The breast augmentation she'd received in high school had been accompanied by a long list of other procedures, none of which made her attractive. Her tight features reminded Bexley of a Barbie doll cooked on hot pavement. From the overabundance of diamonds adorning her neck and digits, it seemed

Amanda had landed the sugar daddy she'd always wanted.

"Oh, this is precious," Amanda sneered. "Bexley Ferguson? Funny, I don't remember seeing the name of the person who ruined my ex on the list."

Five seconds into the treacherous reunion and the gloves were already off. But how did Amanda know about Bexley's failed relationship with Grayson? And why did she think he was "ruined?"

Bexley cocked her head. "That's strange. How does a person not make their own list?"

"She's with me," Brewer interrupted, squeezing Bexley's hand. The gesture was commonly his silent plea for her to "chill."

Amanda set a hand on her hip, eyeing him up and down with a Cheshire cat like grin. "And who are you?"

Brewer squared his jaw. "I'm the guy whose locker you and your ex's friends filled with garbage our sophomore year."

Bexley's heart skipped a beat. She had no idea he'd also been targeted by PS High's infamous bullying squad.

At the same time, Amanda's lips parted and her eyes bulged. "Brewer Hawkins?" Sparks of interest lit her eyes when she smiled. "Oh my god, you look—"

"Bitter?" Bexley finished, filled with a sudden bolt of rage. "Chastised? Way off your radar?"

"I was gonna say…hot," Amanda answered in a breathy voice. "*Crazy* hot. Are you single?"

Brewer laughed in a cold, heartless sound. "Do yourself a favor and stay the hell away from both of us." He promptly led Bexley away, making a direct line toward the bar.

All at once, Brewer's reason for wanting to attend the reunion made perfect sense to Bexley. He wanted to show those who had hurt him that he'd survived…and flourished. "You never mentioned the garbage story before," Bexley said quietly. "I guess that explains why you and Grayson didn't exactly hit it off." She spun back around in Amanda's direction. "Give me two seconds alone with that woman in the parking lot, and I'll—"

Brewer hooked his hand around her forearm. "Save it, Squires. They didn't hurt me back then, and I don't have any repressed feelings about it now. I just really don't have time to pretend with assholes like her." He stepped closer and grasped Bexley's chin in his fingers. "We came here to have a good time. Go get yourself a drink. I'll find Kiersten and Luke."

After laying a mind-scrambling kiss on her lips, he disappeared into the crowd. Feeling a little wobbly on her feet, Bexley joined the long line leading up to the bar. Although it was against Brewer's conditions of release to possess alcohol, there was nothing holding *her* back. Maybe she'd enjoy the night better with a shot of something strong. Better yet, maybe the entire hotel would be wiped out by a meteor.

Minutes later, her stomach dropped to her feet when she spotted Grayson staggering in her direction, glossed eyes piercing her like lasers. "The karma police must despise me," Bexley muttered under her breath.

Once Grayson stood directly in front of her, she was overwhelmed by the stench of alcohol. She had only witnessed him that inebriated one other time, when he was celebrating the conclusion of a big case involving the abduction of a child. Something told her the reason behind that night's binge was something much different. Was Amanda right? Had Bexley done that to him?

"Congratulations on snagging yourself a felon," he slurred. "Hope you've been tested for STDs."

"Don't hold back, Grayson. Tell me how you really feel." Slipping a hand under his armpit, Bexley led him away from the line. "Sounds like it's time for you to call it a night, big guy. Wouldn't want our classmates thinking you became a Class A jerk since high school."

Grayson spun around to seize her arm, eyes narrowed. "You were already sleeping with him while we were still together, weren't you?"

Although there wasn't even a hint of truth to the accusation, she wasn't going to dignify his rant with an answer. She tried twisting away from his painful grip. "Let go, Gray. You're hurting me."

"It makes perfect sense," he continued. "That's why you left. That's why—"

"Get your hand off her," Brewer said in an angry growl, suddenly right behind them.

Bexley spun around to find Kiersten and Luke along with Brewer. She sighed, relieved they'd come to her rescue in that moment. Most of all, she appreciated that Brewer hadn't yanked her away from Grayson like a possessive boyfriend.

Releasing Bexley, Grayson stumbled back. He turned on Brewer with an expression of total rage. "Who do you think you are? She's too damn good for someone like you!"

"You're absolutely right about that, buddy," Brewer agreed, eyeing Bexley. "That's why I'm doing everything in my power to become a better man."

Heat blossomed in Bexley's chest. In that bizarre moment, she realized her feelings for Brewer ran deeper than she realized. She only wished that moment hadn't played out in front of dozens of curious classmates.

"How's that working out for you?" Grayson sneered. "You really believe she's gonna stick around while you're becoming someone's bitch in prison?"

Brewer charged, arm cocked back to take a swing. Bexley quickly wedged herself between the men, holding Brewer an arm's length away. Luke quickly lodged himself in front of Grayson, shaking his head.

"You can't afford to get into a fight with a detective," Bexley warned Brewer. Then she eyed Grayson with contempt. "Even if he's acting like a complete lunatic."

"That's lieutenant to you!" Grayson growled. With a harsh laugh he added, "Someone had to take Baker's place after he killed himself!"

*"Grayson!"* Kiersten snapped, hooking her arm under his. "You need to cool down!"

Wincing, Bexley turned to the crowd. "Okay, show's over, folks. Be sure to tip your server on your way out." Only a few turned away as she took Brewer's hand. "Can we please get out of here before the pits of Hell open all the way up and swallow me whole?"

"I was thinking ribs and beer are more our speed anyway." He lifted his chin in Luke's direction. "You guys in?"

Luke glanced over his shoulder to watch Kiersten lead Grayson away. "Let us know where you end up. We'll probably catch up with you later."

Bexley couldn't get out of there fast enough. Once in the parking lot, she sucked in the cool evening air and turned to Brewer. "Let's make it a standing rule to never attend one of our high school reunions again. Like ever."

"I'm sorry I made you come tonight," he said, pulling her under his arm and kissing her temple. "I always assumed you were popular. I mean, you were the hottest girl in school."

Although Bexley figured they were the obligated words of a boyfriend, she stopped to brush her lips over his. It was her standard way of thanking him without having to say a thing. Brewer deepened the kiss with his standard response of "you're welcome."

Drawing back, Brewer brushed the pad of his thumb across her lips. "Forget ribs. I want you all to myself for the rest of the night. Besides, I have something important I wanna tell you."

Just then, her phone buzzed from the leather clutch Kiersten had provided. She thought she'd felt it vibrate a few times while they were inside, too.

"Hold that thought." With a grunt she retrieved her phone, discovering she'd missed a string of calls from the Currie County Sheriff's Office. Figuring the night couldn't possibly get any worse, she accepted the call.

"Bexley? It's Deputy Danks." He paused, drawing in an audible breath. "There's been an accident."

CHAPTER TWO

The Papaya Springs city mortuary was located in the basement of the city's new hospital. A sense of dread spread through Bexley when the elevator doors opened, exposing an empty, dimly-lit hallway. With every click of her heels on the spotless tile, she began to wish she'd taken Brewer up on his offer to come along even though she'd decided it was time to stop relying on him. With every breath of antiseptic she inhaled, the reality of the situation began to sink in.

Her father was dead.

After ending the call from Deputy Danks, she'd repeated the conversation to Brewer in a monotone voice. He'd looked wary when he asked if she was okay. She'd responded by asking him to take her to identify her father's body.

She followed the signs to the morgue. A young, pretty brunette with kind eyes and a gentle yet firm smile emerged from a set of double doors. She wore a white doctor's coat with a black v-neck blouse underneath and a skirt too short to be seen. "Miss Ferguson?"

"It's Squires," Bexley corrected her.

"I'm Julia Stewart, the Chief Medical Examiner for Papaya Springs." The woman lowered her head. "Please follow me."

They passed through the set of doors to a sterile room with steel coolers and a single body on a gurney, covered by a sheet. Bexley's stomach surged. She wasn't sure if she could smell the stench of death, or if it was only imagined.

The woman gripped the edge of the sheet and paused. "Take a deep breath."

Bexley's shoulders rose with a silent inhale as her father's placid face was exposed. Aside from a massive bruise across his forehead, he hardly looked different from their dinner the night before. In fact, he could've been sleeping. She waited for sadness to overwhelm her, but she felt nothing more than a cold chill from the room's unusually low temperature. "It's him," she muttered. "Captain Dominic Ferguson."

"I'm sorry for your loss," Julia told her. "Would you like a minute alone?"

"That won't be necessary." Bexley tore her eyes away from her father, glancing around the dark room. "Where are his personal effects?"

Moving across the room to a countertop, Julia retrieved a brown leather duffle bag. "This was everything the deputies could find in the vehicle," she told Bexley as she handed it over.

The weight of her father's belongings felt exceptionally heavy in Bexley's hand. She glanced down at the bag, wondering where he could've been headed. He hadn't mentioned a trip at their dinner.

"Is there a certain funeral home you prefer to use?" Julia asked.

"Doesn't matter as long as it offers cremation services." The notion of standing beside a casket while being comforted by strangers made the room spin. Considering the captain was not a religious man, a private service at the cemetery made the most sense. "I was told his time of death was over a dozen hours ago. Why'd it take so long to contact next of kin?"

"From what I understand, there were some problems correctly identifying him at first."

Bexley frowned. His face was perfectly intact. "What kind of problems?"

Once again, Julia offered another kind smile. "You might want to speak to the sheriff."

AS SPEAKING WITH SHERIFF BLAIR WAS ONE OF THE last things Bexley wanted to do on a Saturday night —or ever again for that matter—she was relieved to find only a few deputies on duty, one being her trusted friend, Deputy Danks.

The young, bright-eyed transplant from Virginia rushed toward Bexley and Brewer as they entered the station, a solemn expression on his pale face. "Bex…I'm really sorry about your father."

She dismissed his sympathy with a small shake of her head. "Why did the ME tell me there were problems identifying him?"

Danks gave the other deputy behind the reception desk an uneasy look before turning back to Bexley and Brewer. "Come with me."

He led them to a break room that was bare beyond an old refrigerator and a lightly stocked vending machine. Notices issued by the Sheriff's office were taped to the wall next to fliers on fugitives and missing children. As Bexley and Brewer took chairs at the round table in the center, Danks closed the door. He sat down across from them, looking paler by the second.

"At the time of the accident, your father wasn't carrying any forms of identification. The officers on the scene ran the plates on the two thousand nineteen Benz he was driving, and discovered it was registered to someone by the name of Taylor Hartman. When they contacted Mr. Hartman, he informed them that his plates had recently been stolen off his pickup truck while he was parked in a motel lot outside of L.A. Then the officers ran the VIN number on the sedan driven by your father." Danks paused to clear his throat. "The vehicle was reported as…stolen…from a grocery store parking lot downtown."

Bexley gripped the edge of the table. "I'm sorry. What?"

"The captain was driving a stolen car?" Brewer confirmed, sounding equally confused.

Danks bobbed his chin with a slow nod. "It appears so."

Rubbing at her throbbing temple, Bexley shook

her head. "There's no way." She said it more to herself than anyone in the room. "The captain abhorred criminal activity of any kind. And he had the Caddy. What reason would he have to steal a car?"

"I'm sorry I don't have more answers for you," Danks offered. "I'm sure this is hard to digest."

*More like impossible*, Bexley decided. "Can you run over the facts of his accident one more time?"

After a deep inhale, Danks recited, "He was northbound on one-oh-seven, traveling approximately two miles over the speed limit. It was a single-vehicle accident. The tire marks indicate he wasn't swerving to avoid anything, but rather he veered into a median. They believe he died on impact due to the blunt trauma to his head. The autopsy indicated the cause of the accident was likely due to fatigue as there weren't signs of a heart attack or a stroke, and there weren't any chemicals in his system."

Bexley refused to believe the demise of her father, a decorated officer who had served two tours in Desert Storm, was because he'd been too tired to drive. He thrived on structure, and wouldn't get behind the wheel if he wasn't operating at a hundred percent. "Can I get a copy of the accident report?"

Danks glanced at Brewer before answering, "Are you sure you want to see it?"

"It's the only way I can start to make sense of what happened!" she snapped.

Standing, Danks gave a compliant nod. "They only sent a handwritten summary of the accident, containing everything I told you, along with a note stating the car fob was taken into evidence. As soon as I have their official report, I'll forward it to your office." He attempted a smile. "In the meantime, let me know if there's anything I can do to help."

Bexley and Brewer left the building side-by-side, silently processing the captain's fate. Once seated back inside the passenger's side of her vehicle, Bexley finally opened her father's duffel bag. She found a change of casual clothes, a few toiletries, and nothing more inside. She carefully examined his pale blue polo shirt as if it was hiding secrets.

"Where was he going?" she asked aloud. "What was he doing, driving a stolen car in the middle of the night?"

Brewer climbed into the driver's seat, stopping to squeeze her knee. Although she appreciated that he'd given her space to grieve in her own way rather than codling her, she yearned for more of his touch. "If anyone can figure out what he was up to, it's you."

But when he pressed a kiss to the side of her head, she stiffened and turned away.

"You better call your sister," he said quietly.

---

COCOONED BY BREWER'S HARD CHEST AND BRAWNY arms, Bexley still found it impossible to sleep. She watched the blades of her ceiling fan whirl around as she dissected the facts of her father's accident, and the reasons he could possibly have had for stealing a vehicle. As he hadn't been excessively speeding, he must not've been on the run from someone or something that would call for a quick getaway. The idea that he stole it to make a profit was downright ludicrous. He'd lived a comfortable life, and had recently activated his pension. She could only imagine that he was on his way to perform an illegal act. But what? Could someone have been forcing him to do it against his will?

She couldn't ignore the fact that he'd died just hours after their Christmas dinner. He'd made somewhat of an effort to get along with everyone until he started drilling Brewer about his future. She refused to believe the accident was the direct result of a suicide. He'd been far too arrogant of a man to take his own life. But still…what if he'd been angry over their family discord? What if there was more going on in his life than he'd be willing to disclose to his daughters? What if Bexley's mistreatment of their relationship had pushed him over the edge?

When she'd called Cineste with the news, her little sister had reacted with shock, then genuine grief. Once Cineste's cries became inconsolable, Alex took her phone and asked Bexley what was wrong. Bexley wanted to say, "what's wrong is your girlfriend is crying for a man she once despised," but thought better of it. He suggested they meet for dinner the following night to start arrangements, and offered his "deepest sympathies."

Bexley was still numb. She was beginning to suspect she'd never feel the full impact of losing another parent—even if he hadn't been a good father. Uncovering the reasoning behind his bewildering actions was the only way she could process his death and move forward.

As the sun was coming up, she donned a tank top and yoga pants with tennis shoes. She ran alongside the beach for several miles, hoping to clear her head. It was an exceptionally cold day, even for December, and the low temperature pushed her to run faster. The harder her heart focused on pumping blood, the less likely she was to obsess over the underlying source of her pain. Whatever her father had done was a serious betrayal to his character—to his family. Hadn't he caused them enough agony already?

She eyed the little blue cottage on the beach ahead, tucked beside a wall of rocks, that marked the end of the route she usually ran with Brewer. When she first returned to the area it had been abandoned, but someone had recently been showing it serious TLC. With the help of a new metal roof, shake siding, and sliding doors that opened to a wood patio, it had transformed into the most charming home she'd ever seen. Countless times she'd dreamed of living a simple life in a quiet place like that where she could clear her head with the sound of the ocean coming from her backyard. That morning she yearned to lock herself inside the adorable little house, and hide from the world.

Instead of returning to Brewer, she headed into the office. She hadn't received anything from Danks, and suspected it would take a day or two before she'd see her father's accident report. The best way to quiet her unease would be to throw herself into work.

Her fingers mindlessly clicked the pen from Cineste with the *"be a quick wit"* inscription. Her first instinct was to dig into her father's personal affairs, starting with his email. The meticulous military man who'd raised them was bound to keep a journal of accounts and passwords in his home office. She'd never set foot inside the home he'd bought near the city's largest beach with Hillary, his last ex-wife, but Bexley imagined he would've insisted on having a stately desk with a computer setup similar to what he'd had when she was in high school. The wall behind him had been lined with plaques and awards that told the story of a sailor dedicated to protecting his country. Meanwhile, there wasn't a single picture of his family to be seen.

Deciding she'd grab coffee and a breakfast sandwich along the way, she powered her new desktop computer down. Right as she stood, she heard a woman call out, "Hello?"

Bexley strode out to the reception area, finding a tall, voluptuous blonde in a modestly cut designer dress and heels. The fashionable young woman's stance alluded assertiveness as her pale blue, cartoonish-sized eyes scanned up and down Bexley's worn running outfit and tousled ponytail. "Are you a private investigator?"

"You'll have to forgive me," Bexley said. "My evening gown is at the cleaner's."

The woman gave a dry laugh. "I didn't expect you to be open on a Sunday, but I noticed the lights were on."

"Like Cage the Elephant says, ain't no rest for the wicked, and money don't grow on trees." Remembering she was likely speaking with a potential client, Bexley forced a friendly smile. She really needed to work on her people skills. "Can I help you?"

The woman squared her chin while offering her hand. "Elizabeth Ricci."

A flicker of recognition struck Bexley as she gave the woman's hand a firm shake. She'd heard the name Ricci, but couldn't place it. "Bexley Squires."

Elizabeth withdrew her hand and folded her arms over her stomach, grinning. "A good friend of mine claims you're exceptionally good at what you do."

"Your friend sounds smart."

"I'd like to hire you to help me out of an unfortunate situation." Elizabeth arched a perfectly sculpted brow. "I'd pay extra for your discretion."

"Discretion is already figured into my services." Dollar signs flashed before Bexley's eyes. Based on the woman's flawless appearance, she was undoubtedly one of the city's elite. Considering she was younger than Bexley, at the very least she was an heiress to someone with a fat bank account. Bexley turned sideways, gesturing toward her office. "Come have a seat while you tell me about your situation."

As they re-entered her office, Bexley caught the woman giving the small space the same kind of scrutiny she'd given Bexley's workout attire. Bexley wasn't mentally prepared to move into J.J.'s larger office quite yet. She'd spent more than she should've in updating the office equipment, and was saving to give the building a thorough facelift. Until then, she was stuck with dark paneling and popcorn ceilings that resembled something straight out of a 70s noir.

Elizabeth lowered into the chair across from Bexley. "What I'm about to tell you doesn't leave this room," she warned.

"Of course," Bexley agreed.

"I was robbed last night."

Bexley leaned in, resting her forearms on her desk. "Did you call the police?"

"No. I was robbed by someone I met on an anonymous hook up website for wealthy people." Elizabeth squared her shoulders and shook her sleek golden mane. "Before you judge me, Miss Squires, you have no idea how hard it is to find someone who likes me for who I am, and isn't afraid of my father. It's easier to maintain something anonymous with casual sex."

"No judgments here," Bexley assured her. She knew all too well of the consequences that could come with trusting the wrong man after her experience with Dean Halliwell. And an intimidating father? Been there, done that, bought the overpriced souvenir. "You don't have his name?"

"He told me to call him Brad after I made the comment that he reminded me of a younger Brad Pitt. And he called me Bella for beautiful." She briefly closed her eyes. "I know how this must sound to you." Her expression hardened. "I normally don't invite guys I've met on the site back to my place, but this one seemed different. I was foolish enough to believe there was something substantial forming between us when he suggested we meet up for a fifth time, even though I still didn't know his name. I'd started to develop real feelings for the guy. Not just because of the sex, even though it was pretty phenomenal. Clean cut, well dressed, civilized and polite—he was a real gentleman. All the signs were there that he came from old money like he claimed. I thought maybe..." She dabbed an expertly manicured fingertip to the corner of one eye, then the other. "Forget it. None of that matters." Her lips pressed into a tight line. "The bastard must've rifled through my condo after I fell asleep. From what I can tell so far, he stole somewhere in the neighborhood of two point five million worth."

"That's a hefty chunk of change." Bexley leaned back in her chair, barely suppressing a whistle. "Elizabeth, are you absolutely sure you don't want to get the police involved?"

Once again, Elizabeth's lips pressed together as her brow wrinkled. "My father would disown me if the truth came out. I wouldn't give the bastard who cleaned me out that kind of satisfaction." She leaned closer, eyes ablaze. "This man took something from me that's much more valuable than my father's fortune. Plus he humiliated me. I'm willing to pay you whatever it takes to find this son of a bitch, and nail his balls to the wall."

Although Bexley couldn't imagine what could possibly be more valuable than two million dollars, she nodded. She could empathize with the desire for justice that was evident in Elizabeth's tone. "I'm going to need full access to your dating account, an itemized list of everything that's missing, and any little detail you can tell me about 'Brad'. What brand of clothing he wore, what kind of car he drove, anything that could help us track him down." She plucked her business card from a small box on the corner of her desk, and handed it over. "Email the information to me, and I'll get to work on tracking him down right away. My hourly rate—"

"I'll pay you fifty grand up front," Elizabeth blurted. "Another fifty once my possessions are returned." She raised one eyebrow. "Like I said, he stole something more valuable than money."

A reply stuck in Bexley's throat. A hundred thousand dollars? Who was this woman's father, and what did the man steal that set her off? With that kind of cash, Bexley could remodel the office down to its studs, and have enough leftover to install a Prosecco fountain in the reception area. She was ready to accept the offer when they heard the front door to the building bounce shut.

"There's no hiding from me, Squires." The sexy

roll of Brewer's voice drew closer as he added, "You forget I always know exactly what's going through that beautiful head." He appeared in her doorway with a crooked grin and a cup of coffee in hand. In fitted blue jeans and the exceptionally soft gray hoodie with "still plays with blocks" written beneath the drawing of a car engine, rich brown hair damp from a shower, magnetism seeped from his pores. Had Bexley been alone, she may've caved to the impulse of jumping his gorgeous bones.

When he spotted Elizabeth, his expression flattened. He began to back away. "Sorry, I—"

Elizabeth quickly stood on her designer heels. "It's okay, I was on my way out."

"I'll wait out here," Brewer offered, seemingly embarrassed the way he side-eyed Bexley and tucked his chin before closing the door.

"Sorry about that." Bexley stood to shake Elizabeth's hand once more. "Thank you, Miss Ricci. I'll do everything in my power to find this man, and return everything he stole from you."

"I'll return first thing tomorrow with your first check and the information you requested," Elizabeth promised.

Pulse thrumming with excitement, Bexley smiled. "I'll have a contract ready for you to sign."

Elizabeth tilted her head toward the doorway. "Do yourself a favor, and don't trust guys like him. The best looking ones tend to burn the deepest."

She spun around and promptly left Bexley gaping after her.

Brewer returned to her doorway, frowning. "What was she doing here?"

From the tone of his voice, Bexley suspected he was quite familiar with Elizabeth. She only hoped it wasn't the same way in which he was familiar with Bexley. "Old friend of yours?"

"B, that's the daughter of Mattia Ricci. The mob boss? He owns half this town."

"Guess that would explain the royalty vibe I was getting from her."

Warning bells clambered inside her head. Her battles with a beloved movie star, the powerful city's mayor and the district attorney, and most recently, Grayson's boss, had nearly cost her everything. Was she ready to get involved with mob royalty?

Eyes pained with worry, Brewer gripped her chin in his fingers. "Hey. You alright?"

"I will be after a shower." While snatching the cup of coffee from his hands, she brushed her lips over his, smiling. "Then I'm taking you out for brunch—somewhere way over-priced."

# CHAPTER THREE

As promised, Elizabeth Ricci stopped by Stronghold Investigations early Monday morning with her account username/password combo for the dating site, an itemized list of objects taken from her condominium, and a $50,000 check. In addition, she included facts about her nameless hook up that didn't extend too far beyond his looks and ability to smooth talk his way through any situation. The "blond-haired, blue-eyed hottie in his late twenties" Elizabeth described was the quintessential California surfer.

Having blown off dinner with Cineste and Alex the night before to research Elizabeth's background, Bexley eyed the young woman with a new perspective. The mob princess was twenty-four—fifteen years younger than her only sibling, a half-sister. After several surgical enhancements, she'd gained a hefty following of impressionable young girls on social media, and dabbled in modeling. It seemed logical the "friend" who had sent Elizabeth her way was Temperance Rose, the reality star who'd become more than a causal acquaintance of Bexley's, as the two attractive women appeared together in several pictures Elizabeth had posted. Bexley suspected that Kiersten would admire Elizabeth's black pencil skirt and white with black polka dotted blouse as well as the diligent way she'd styled her platinum blond locks into a complicated braid. Bexley also suspected Elizabeth was accustomed to getting everything she wanted, adding another layer of pressure to locate the thief.

Red had prepared a contract per Bexley's instructions, and she notarized Elizabeth's signature while Bexley supervised over her shoulder. There was something unusual in the way Bexley's new employee addressed Elizabeth and bounced around on the sparkling pumps she wore with blue jeans, one of her typical nerd-themed t-shirts, and a long emerald sweater.

Once everything was settled, Elizabeth cut a sharp look in Red's direction. Bexley was sure she was scrutinizing Red's flamboyant style the way she'd snubbed Bexley for wearing cheap leggings. "As I told Miss Squires, I expect my case to be handled with the highest level of discretion."

"I hired Miss Casey because she's a true professional," Bexley assured her in a sharp tone. "She understands the importance of confidentiality with our clients. I wouldn't expect anything less from my employees."

Red nodded with too much enthusiasm. "She's totally right. I'm sorry if I'm acting strangely. It's just that...I saw pictures of the Star Wars themed party you threw for your friend Max, and it was the most amazing thing I'd ever seen." Red steepled her hands together. "May I ask you something? Were those Storm Trooper costumes from the actual movie set? Because I have to say they were—"

With a choked laugh, Bexley nudged Red aside. "Total discretion," she repeated, still holding Elizabeth's stare.

As the coiffed blonde pulled out of Stronghold's parking lot in a white convertible Lamborghini—interestingly enough bearing dealer plates—Red squawked with strange noises at Bexley's side.

"Er my...holy...for the love...I cannot believe this is my life. Are you kidding me, boss lady?

You've been hired by the PS Princess?" She held the check up to the light. "This baby is probably embossed with real gold."

"You cannot mention a word of this to another soul," Bexley warned, grabbing the check from Red's bedazzled fingernails. She studied the foil print for a moment, wondering if Red could be right. The weight of the paper alone was three times that of a normal bank check, and the embossed letters did seem exceptionally sparkly. "And I don't want to hear you refer to her as that ever again. As fitting as it may be, it's unprofessional."

"You're right," Red sank into the chair behind the receptionist's desk. "I'm sorry."

Bexley scanned over Elizabeth's list. "Who spends two hundred grand on a key?"

"Maybe it unlocks her ten million dollar diary, handmade by monks in Tibet."

"Is that really a thing?"

Snorting, Red opened her palms at her sides. "All I know is rich people have a history of blowing their money on ridiculously moronic things. I once read someone paid over a hundred k for a lock of Elvis Presley's hair."

Bexley rifled through the papers—lightly

fragrant with the smell of roses—and handed Red the neatly penned information about the hook up website. "Log into her account, and see if you can triangulate this guy's location. I want a hard copy of whatever you're able to see on him, including every last one of their conversations."

Sheet of paper in hand, Red lowered behind her desk. "I'm on it."

Bexley went into her office to study the list. It continued on with each outrageously priced item more ridiculous than the last.

*$150k diamond handbag*

*$200k gold key*

*$270k ruby heart-shaped necklace*

*$300k miniature greenhouse*

*$390k diamond watch*

*$600k designer stilettos*

Disgusted, Bexley dropped the paper and watched it float down to her desk. What was a miniature greenhouse, and why was it so expensive? What did a person even do with something like that?

Her cell phone buzzed with an incoming call from Cineste. Since she was already in hot water for cancelling the night before, she didn't dare blow her sister off a second time.

"I'm working, Cin," she answered. "Can I call you back later?"

"No, you can't!" Cineste barked. "We have to decide what to do with dad and all his things! Your stupid clients can wait!"

Grumbling to herself, Bexley checked the time on the analog clock that came with her office. "Fine. Can you meet me at his house for lunch?" She'd been putting off the trip there anyway. "I'll bring Pollo's."

"My last class for the day is done at noon," Cineste said, all at once calm. "I can be there by twelve thirty. And bring more tacos for the guys. Alex wants to be there for all of this, and Brewer should be too. I know things weren't great with you and dad, but I think it's important we both have emotional support throughout the process. At some point you'll realize he was a good man who tried to be a good father in the end."

Ending the call, Bexley shook her head. Since she had yet to tell Cineste the sordid details of their father's accident, she had a feeling her sister would be the one who needed emotional support.

She dialed Brewer's work number, knowing he

was likely under some car, and always left his cell phone in the office. She was grateful to hear him answer with the name of his shop rather than one of his moody employees.

"I need someone to take a look under my hood," she purred in an ultra feminine, sing-song voice. "Would you have time, like, over the noon hour?"

Onto her act, Brewer let out a husky laugh. "Sorry, sweetheart, but that kind of maintenance is reserved for my girlfriend."

She was going to have to work a little harder on undercover personalities. Her cheeks warmed as she switched to her normal voice. "I'm actually calling because Cineste seems to think it's urgent we sort through the captain's worldly possessions and plan how we're going to stick him in the ground. Wanna spend your lunch break suffering along with me?"

"I...uh..." he stammered. His voice became faint like he was pulling the phone away from his mouth. She thought she even heard him mutter a curse word. There was a weighted pause, then, "I wish I could make that work, but I can't. Sorry, B. Can you reschedule for another time?"

His vague reply struck her as odd, as if he was deliberately hiding something. It didn't help that since the moment they decided to become a couple, she'd been harboring a smidgen of jealousy because of the effect he had on women.

"Hot date with your maid?" She needed to start asserting her independence again. It was only a matter of time until he wouldn't be around. "You know what? Don't worry about it. I'm capable of handling Cineste's antics on my own."

"I'd be there if I could," he swore, sounding deeply remorseful. "I hope you know that." There was a smile in his voice when he said, "How 'bout I come by your place tonight? I'll order Hawaiian pizza from that place you love, and have a bottle of Prosecco waiting on ice. You can tell me all about your meeting with Cineste while I give you a long massage. I already know the situation is going to make you tense."

Her ovaries quaked with the well-meaning offer. The mere idea of his strong hands kneading her muscles stole her breath. The man was practically the perfect boyfriend. Whatever personal reason he had for not coming along shouldn't have bothered her. But it did. And it was time she started letting go.

"I'll be working late tonight," she told him. "Elizabeth Ricci's case is going to have me tied up for a while. I'll see if you're around…when I have time." Before he could object, she hung up.

---

It was around 12:40 by the time Bexley parked next to Cineste's car in their father's driveway. While married to Hillary, he had relocated to the two-story, Spanish colonial revival style home nestled in a clean, quiet neighborhood three blocks from where Bexley had hung out with her friends on the beach in high school. The briny smell of the ocean and screaming of seagulls released a floodgate of unwanted memories. Too many involving Grayson. It angered her that the split with Grayson couldn't have been amicable so they could stay friends. It certainly didn't help that she also thought of him when she stopped by the beloved taco joint that had also been her mom's favorite. Snatching the greasy bag filled with tacos, she slipped from her SUV and slammed the door as Cineste and Alex came out of the house.

"At least you're already in a great mood," Cineste commented dryly.

"I don't exactly have time for this," Bexley

grumbled, turning to shove their lunch at her sister. "Let's get it over with."

Frowning, Cineste clasped the bag in her fingers. "We tried going inside to get a head start, but the front and back doors are all locked." She eyed Bexley's empty hands. "Where's the key?"

"You're joking, right? Cin, the last time I visited any of dad's houses was two wives ago."

"I thought the morgue gave you his stuff."

The dull pang of an oncoming headache stretched across Bexley's forehead. "His stuff didn't include keys of any kind."

Cineste clicked her tongue. "Then why'd you want to meet here?"

"I'm sure he kept a key somewhere like he did when we were little." Pushing her irritation aside, Bexley stormed past her sister. "He was a creature of habit." *The kind of creature that made Dr. Jekyll turn into Hyde,* she thought to herself.

She bent over the landscaping surrounding the front door, turning over every rock she could find. Soon Cineste and Alex were beside her, doing the same. The unopened bag of tacos rested near Cineste's feet.

Bexley cleared her throat. "We should talk

about what we're gonna do with him. Any objections to cremation and a grave-side gathering?"

"Oh my god!" Cineste cried, popping back up to her feet. "You make it sound like we're putting down an old pet! He should have a proper military burial!"

"Can't we just find someone to play a trumpet and shoot off some guns?" As much as she hated to break the news to her sister about their father's indiscretions, she was tired of Cineste playing him up to be a saint who deserved to be buried with honor. "I'm sorry if I'm not more sympathetic to his situation, but he wasn't the good person you're building him up to be!"

Cineste set her hands on her hips. "You know what, Bex? I think it's best if you just leave the planning up to me. If we did it your way, you'd probably throw him in a cigar box and toss it alongside the highway!"

They were interrupted by a gravelly voice from directly behind where they stood. "Put your hands up where I can see them," the man ordered. "All three of ya. Nice and easy, now. Don't be tryin' anything stupid."

Goosebumps broke out along Bexley's arms. She

followed the stranger's instructions before slowly pivoting around. She was met by the narrowed gaze of an elderly, rain-thin gentleman with deep wrinkles covering his face, and very few strands of snow white hair combed over his liver-spotted head. He wore slippers and pajamas beneath a robe.

Bexley noted with bemusement that the gun he held was 100% rubber. Huffing, she dropped her arms at her sides. "Planning to beat each of us silly with that, oldtimer?"

The man lowered the fake gun. "Figured you were a bunch of meth-heads, lookin' for somethin' to steal. But ya look harmless. What business do ya have, pokin' around my neighbors' yard?"

"Our father lived here," Bexley explained. "He died in a car accident a couple days ago. We're here to go through his things."

The old man raised the fake gun. Bexley was starting to believe he thought it was real. "Try again. Max and Shelly may be a couple of weirdos, but they're hardly a day older than the three of ya."

"Max and Shelly?" Cineste repeated, hands held in the air. "We're looking for Dominic Ferguson. He bought this place several years ago with his ex-wife, Hillary."

"Ya mean the captain?" the man asked, eyes narrowed. "Shoot…he hasn't lived here in months."

Bexley turned, throwing her sister a hard look. "Imagine that. Father of the Year failed to mention to either one of us that he'd moved."

"Stop talking about him like that!" Cineste snarled.

Alex stepped between the sisters to address the neighbor. "Do you have any idea where the captain might've moved?"

The man scratched his head. "Damned if I know." With a great exhale, he dropped the toy gun in his gaping robe pocket. "I suggest you move along before I call the cops. Real sorry about your daddy, but you're trespassing."

"No need for that," Alex answered, exposing a palm. "We'll leave peacefully."

With a child-like whimper, Cineste trotted back to her car.

Bexley dropped her head back and rolled her eyes. Her sister had become a different person since they'd rescued her from Alex's evil father and his cronies. The Cineste she'd grown up with despised their father for controlling every aspect of their lives.

"She knows he wasn't perfect," Alex said beside

her. "She was still hoping you'd get over your shit so you guys could be a family again."

"He couldn't have been any further from perfect." Squeezing the bridge of her nose, she glanced down at the driveway. "Alex, there's something I need to tell her about the accident." Swallowing hard, she met his gaze. "The captain was driving a stolen car when he died."

His eyebrows shot up. "For real?"

"He even went to the trouble of stealing a different set of license plates. I'm waiting for the sheriff's office to send me a copy of the accident report. I think there may be more going on with him than any of us were aware."

Whistling, Alex ran his fingers through his short brown hair. He then glanced to where Cineste sat in the car, arms folded, staring straight ahead. "She's gonna freak."

"I know." Bexley sighed. "Maybe it's best if you tell her. She thinks I flat out despised him."

Alex threw her a hard stare. "Don't you?"

Unable to provide him with an answer they'd both believe, Bexley simply walked away.

# CHAPTER FOUR

Back at Stronghold Investigations, Red ambushed Bexley by throwing the door open as she reached for the handle. Her pixie-like face was as animated as Bexley had ever seen.

"I have good news, boss lady!" As she handed Bexley a stack of papers, she smacked her bubble gum. "This thief is a skilled mo-fo. He did a commendable job of covering his tracks except for the third time when he demanded to meet up with Elizabeth immediately. I was able to pinpoint his location to a high end cafe a block from her condo. Either he knew where she was living before she brought him there, or their hook up was truly serendipitous."

Feeling a rush of adrenaline, Bexley held up a

picture of an attractive blonde man with great bone structure, sweetheart lips, and dreamy blue eyes. "This him?"

Red snorted. "Him and about a dozen other guys, according to various dating sites. I ran the picture through a reverse image search and it multiplied like a Gremlin in water. Seems we've found ourselves a bonafide con artist."

Bexley found it odd that someone with Elizabeth's resources wouldn't have thought to run any kind of background check on men she agreed to meet. Especially when it sounded like a simple enough procedure. "If these other dating sites aren't anonymous, is there any way you can track down other women who might've met up with him?"

"I can sure try."

"While you're at it, create a profile for me on a few of the same sites. Give me a false identity, and play up my assets. Make me sound disgustingly wealthy. Maybe we can snag this slimy thief ourselves."

Red's cherry lips parted with a wide smile. "Oooo…I can use the picture you were tagged in from your reunion! You look *way* fierce… modelesque even."

Bexley blanched. She wasn't into social media,

and only vaguely understood what being "tagged" meant. "I was tagged in something from that dumpster fire?"

"It's a great picture, I swear."

If Grayson's ex had posted it, Bexley could only imagine the accompanying caption. With a shake of her head, she decided she didn't want to know any more. "Do you have the address for this cafe?"

Red shuffled the papers and plucked one from the bottom of the stack. "It's about a forty minute drive from here."

Bexley took the sheet back, and held it against her chest with the others. "Good work, Red. I'm going to head there now, see if I can find someone who recognizes him. While I'm gone, run a check of police records to see if there are any reports of other robberies with the same kind of circumstances."

"Wait!" Red darted back to her desk to retrieve more papers sitting beneath her wide, curved monitor. "I almost forgot…these came in on the fax machine a few minutes ago." With a cautious look, she handed them over to Bexley. "It's the report on your dad."

Without giving it a glance, Bexley added it to the paperwork she already held. She wasn't sure how she'd feel about the details of the accident, and she didn't want Red to witness whatever emotions it might stir up. "Thanks. Let me know if you find anything on our buddy 'Brad'." She paused, unsure how deep she wanted to involve her employee in her personal business. The captain's most recent ex-wife might know where Bexley's father had been living, but Bexley didn't want to speak with Hillary just yet. For starters, they weren't exactly friendly. "If you have extra time, check the county records to see if Dominic William Ferguson recently bought a new house in the area. I guess he may've been renting something instead."

Red threw her a sympathetic smile. "Will do, Bex."

Bexley detested the sadness in her employee's voice. She didn't want anyone's empathy. Not when it was connected to a parent who had been nothing but cold and negligent. She put off reading the accident report until she was sitting behind the wheel of her SUV.

As far as police paperwork went, it was pretty standard. The summary was almost verbatim of what Deputy Danks had recited to Bexley. There was an amendment to the original report, including her father's name and date of birth, and a brief explanation of the unusual circumstances behind the vehicle he was driving. She noted the names of the two men who had been victims of the stolen car and stolen plates, intending to track them down. She was desperate for any little detail that would clue her into the captain's behaviors.

Her heart skipped when she noticed one important fact that Deputy Danks had failed to mention. Or perhaps, for one reason or another, Danks hadn't been informed by the officers on the scene. Most important was the fact that someone had tried to erase the entry, perhaps with white-out. But when she held the paper up to the light, she was able to read the redacted information with some difficulty.

It was the phone number of a witness.

Her fingers trembled as she dialed the number. Though it rang without an answer, the voicemail provided Bexley with the information she'd been hoping for.

The witness to her father's accident now had a name.

THE 770 FIX CAFE WAS A TRENDY FUSION OF industrial and feminine, featuring rustic pallet ceilings, monochromatic brick walls, and delicate chandeliers. Electronic tablets accompanied every seat at the granite bar top along with charging ports and little shelves intended for cell phones. The sublime aroma of baked goods struck Bexley's senses the moment she walked inside, reminding her empty stomach that the tacos had been abandoned.

A majority of the dozen or so patrons were housewives of the neighborhood's elite residents. The dead giveaway wasn't just their hundred dollar yoga pants with brand name tank tops and tennis shoes—they also donned several carat diamonds that dripped in unabashed glory from their earlobes and wedding ring fingers. They casually sipped on drinks and carried on conversations without seeming to have a care in the world, some with high-end strollers at their side. Bexley all at once felt transparent in trendy blue jeans, a gray moto jacket, her go-to white button down blouse, and gray ankle boots. She may as well have worn a name badge declaring her to be the help.

A slender barista in the cafe's black uniform, pale blond hair brushed into a high ponytail, greeted Bexley with an enthusiastic smile. Her tanned skin had the youthful glow of a high schooler, which was plausible as they'd be out on break for the holidays. "Welcome to Seven-Seventy. My name's Rachel. What can we make fresh for you today?"

Glancing at the complex menu written in painstakingly perfect handwriting on the chalkboard, Bexley shrugged. "Can I get a blueberry muffin and a cappuccino?"

"Of course. Hot or iced?"

Accustomed to grabbing generic coffee from gas stations, Bexley frowned. "Hot—both the muffin and the drink."

The girl giggled. "What size cappuccino?"

"Something with enough caffeine to energize an elephant."

Giggling a little harder, Rachel started poking at the screen on the counter in front of her. "Extra grande it is. And what type of muffin? We have vegan, gluten free, vegan/gluten free—"

"Just a regular one…with real eggs and flour."

Rachel looked up at Bexley with a wide grin stretching over her bronzed cheeks. "If that's everything, your order comes to twenty-five dollars."

Bexley's jaw dropped. "Exactly how big is that extra grande?"

Again, Rachel giggled. "You said you wanted something big enough for an elephant."

"I have a quick question for you." Before fishing her wallet out from her handbag, Bexley snagged the picture of "Brad," and held it out for the girl to see. "Do you recognize this guy?"

Rachel took the picture from Bexley's fingers, squinting at it. "Yeah, I've seen him around."

"Do you happen to know his name?" Bexley was certain someone with his track record wasn't likely to give out his real name, but it was worth a shot. She'd give anything to sink her teeth into a solid lead.

"I think he said it was Tim. Or maybe it was Jim."

"Have you seen him more than once? Do you remember the last time he stopped in?"

The girl shrugged one shoulder. "I've seen him a handful of times. I just remember he usually came alone."

"Usually?"

"Once he came in with one of our regulars. I got the feeling they were on a date. They were super flirty with each other, and she kept touching his arm. It was weird, because I always thought she was married. She wears a massive diamond ring."

"Do you know this regular's name, and how I might get in touch with her?"

"Sorry. I suck at names." Rachel flashed a dramatic frown. "I have enough to remember with homework, you know?"

Could the woman in question be Elizabeth? Honoring her client's insistence on complete secrecy with her case, Bexley ruled out showing the girl a picture. "Can you describe her for me?"

Rachel's eyes darted to one side. "Shorter than me, hair a darker shade of brown than yours, maybe part Asian. Gorgeous. She's younger than my parents—probably somewhere in her early thirties. The first time I saw her, I wondered if she was an actress. But I think she's some kind of big-shot lawyer. I once complimented her on a cute pink suit she was wearing, and she said she was hoping to 'woo' a jury."

The woman she described was clearly not Elizabeth. "Have you seen her come in since they were last seen together?"

"She was just here this morning," Rachel answered, standing a little taller. "I think a little after six—a few minutes after we open. She usually stops in two or three days every week."

"Always around the same time?"

"I think so."

"Do you work again this week?"

Rachel huffed. "My parents own this place, and they're making me work here every day before school until I pay off the cost to fix my Mercedes. The accident wasn't even my fault."

*Rough life,* Bexley thought as she exchanged cash for her coffee and muffin. "Thanks for your time, Rachel. You've been super helpful." She handed the girl a business card. "I'll try to catch her tomorrow. If for any reason I miss her, please have her give me a call. Tell her it's urgent."

Rachel glanced down at the card. "You're a private investigator? You don't look like one. You're way too pretty."

"Must be the new shampoo I'm using," Bexley mused with a wink.

In the cafe's small parking lot, she set her monster cup of coffee over the two cupholders and jammed the muffin in her mouth while checking her phone for messages. She'd just missed a return call from the witness of her father's accident. She quickly redialed. "Christine Woodland?"

"Who *is* this?" a soft-spoken woman answered.

"Sorry I didn't leave a message earlier. You don't know me, but my name is Bexley Squires. The police told me you're the only witness to my father's accident. The Benz you saw crash?"

"Oh…I'm sorry. I didn't realize they'd figured out who the guy was."

"I'm hoping you'd have a few minutes to meet with me, Christine. I have some questions about that night."

"Sorry, but, um, my schedule is already tight the way it is." Christine's words came out in a rush, as if she was searching for any valid excuse. "I attend beauty school by day, and waitress at Sneaky Pete's Cove by night. Plus I'm a single mom. I barely have any time to spend with my kids." She clicked her tongue impatiently. "Can't you get a copy of my statement from the police?"

"I've already seen it. I have a few more questions." Bexley wasn't going to give in that easily. She sensed something else was making the girl hesitant. "Isn't Sneaky Pete's Cove that tiki bar right on the beach down the road from Papaya Springs Royal? I could stop by while you're on a break."

"I don't know," Christine stammered. "I—"

"Please," Bexley begged, trying her best to emulate the voice of a grieving daughter. "I need to hear you describe that night first hand. It's just so hard to believe my daddy is really gone!"

"Okay, fine," Christine relented. "Meet me at Sneaky Pete's at eight o'clock sharp. I can only give you ten minutes, tops."

"Thanks, Christine. I'll see you then." Feeling a spark of hope, Bexley ended the call.

As Bexley pulled up in front of Stronghold Investigations one last time before calling it a day, she spotted Kiersten striding toward her, jaw held tight. Bexley's shoulders sank. Either Brewer or Cineste must've brought her up to speed.

Kiersten had an innocent, angelic look about her in a feminine dress in a white and light blue pattern that swirled at her ankles. It was a sharp contrast to her accessories of a black biker coat and laced leather boots, but perfectly matched the bohemian style of her natural blond waves and oversized cat's eye sunglasses.

"Save your breath," Bexley warned as she slipped out from her vehicle. She wagged a finger at her stylish friend. "You know exactly how I felt about the captain."

Kiersten's tongue clicked behind her glossy pink lips. "Still doesn't make it right that I had to hear about it from your sister." She removed her sunglasses, revealing the pain in her expression. "Am I even allowed to ask how you're dealing?"

"You'll have to forgive me if this sounds crass, but I'm only losing sleep over it because he was driving a stolen car when he died."

"Get out!" Kiersten's eyes rounded. "Are we talking about the same man who made you do community service for a month because he mistakenly thought you'd stolen a candy bar in the first grade?"

"I'm not surprised Cineste didn't mention it." Bexley wiped a weary hand over her face. Maybe Alex hadn't told Cineste like she'd hoped. "We're not exactly seeing eye-to-eye on the captain's demise."

"I gathered that when she called. She made a point of telling me she'd made the arrangements for the grave-side service with military honors on Thursday. She sounded incredibly bitter. Wouldn't mention you by name—kept saying 'my sister' like you were the devil incarnate."

Cineste certainly didn't waste any time making plans, Bexley decided. At least her sister had agreed on the size and location of the service. "I guess I should be grateful she sent you by to fill me in on the details."

"Actually, she's not the one who sent me. I came by to check on you as a favor. To…Gray."

Bexley's blood boiled. "After the scene he caused at the reunion the other night?" She set a hand on her hip and scowled. "It was hardly a minute after he was ready to fight Brewer that the sheriff's office called me in to ID my father's corpse."

Kiersten let out a dramatic sigh and rolled her eyes. "He knows he royally screwed up. That's why he asked me to stop by." She inclined her chin. "He's hurt that you've moved on because he still loves you, Bex. He still hopes that you'll change your mind, and eventually go back to him."

"That's not going to happen."

"I know, I know. As much as I adored having my two besties together, I've started to understand why you're better off with Brewer. The guy lets you do your thing without smothering you with worry, or asking you to be someone else. It just sucks that he's going off to jail soon."

Like Bexley needed the reminder. "You need to encourage Grayson to move on."

"I'll try my best to help him let go." With a

sincere expression, she took Bexley's hands in hers. "Speaking of smothering, if I promise not to do that either, can Luke and I stop by your apartment later tonight? We can grab whatever you guys want for dinner—even ribs from that sketchy place Brewer seems to be obsessed with."

"Actually, I was thinking of hitting Sneaky Pete's Cove. I heard their fish tacos are supposed to be the best in Papaya Springs. You could meet me there… around six." She didn't want word getting back to Cineste that she was investigating their father's death, and it would give her enough time to socialize with her friends before she met with the witness.

"What about Brewer?" Kiersten asked.

"I'm sure he'll be there too," Bexley lied. She had no intention of extending an invitation, even though he'd called and sent several texts since they spoke before lunch. She'd decided it was best for both of them to give each other more space. Leaving a girlfriend behind while serving time may only make things harder for Brewer.

Red threw the door open just then, waving a paper through the air. "I found it! I have the address where your dad was living!"

Bexley frowned in Kiersten's direction. "The work of the captain's daughter is never done."

CHAPTER FIVE

The captain had been holed up in a shoddy apartment complex on the farthest end of the East Side, known to be inhabited by crackheads and prostitutes. From the looks of the ancient building situated at the end of an empty block—patchy shingles, broken windows boarded up, siding in need of serious repair—it was one missing brick away from being deemed uninhabitable. An eerie quiet fell over the dark neighborhood. Either it had been abandoned because of declining conditions, or the area residents were resting up for another night of bad decisions and illicit activities. Then again, maybe everyone was smart enough not to visit the neighborhood at night.

Bexley stared at the building from her SUV,

baffled. What could've driven her father to such extremes? Bexley didn't think he displayed any signs of a drug addiction. Had he stolen the car because he'd somehow lost all his money, or were both situations pieces of a puzzle?

Swallowing her pride, she called her father's ex-wife. It had been several months since Bexley had reached out to the adulterer. She was somewhat relieved to hear Hillary's recorded voice directing her to leave a message.

"Hillary? It's Bexley. I'm not sure if you've heard the news…my father was killed in a car accident over the weekend. I know you two weren't on the best terms, but I was hoping you'd have some insight into his living situation. Can you please call me as soon as you get this?"

She gave the building one last glance before driving away. She'd made numerous regretful decisions since becoming a PI, but she wasn't about to add venturing through the ominous neighborhood on her own to the list.

SNEAKY PETE'S COVE PROVED TO BE A POPULAR hangout for college students taking full advantage of the taco special. The outdoor patio was crammed with coeds already intoxicated from the restaurant's other special of the night—$2 tap beers. Among strings of twinkling lights, palm trees decorated with festive holiday decor, and sky blue umbrellas wrapped up for the night, shouted conversations and bright laughter trumped the sounds of upbeat pop music and the roaring ocean in the dark distance.

With a bemused smile, Bexley remembered a similar scene while attending NYU—minus the beach, of course. Her friends had dubbed the popular gathering place "the meat market" as it was where everyone went for random hookups. Ironically, it was there she'd met Jack Squires, her short-lived husband who'd saved her from using her father's surname. From a young age, she'd been eager to distance herself from the captain's legacy. She was beginning to wonder if it had been some kind of survival instinct. Maybe even the start of her destiny as an investigator.

Irritation rumbled through her core when she spotted Kiersten and Luke headed toward the establishment—Brewer was close behind. Had Kiersten called him? Worse yet, was he somehow tracking her?

"Two minutes alone with me, beautiful, and I'll make that frown turn upside down," a baritone voice rumbled from behind.

Bexley pivoted around to find a well-built kid with wavy blond hair, beautiful blue eyes, and the baby face of a naive teenager. She doubted he was old enough to buy the frothy tap beer in his hand. "With that pick-up line, I'm going to assume you still live in your mom's basement."

Brewer was suddenly at Bexley's side, throwing the kid an intimidating scowl. "In two minutes, it'll be past your bedtime," he said.

Grumbling to himself, the kid sulked away. Bexley's anger dissipated the moment Brewer's soft lips pressed to her forehead, and his scent surrounded her like a much-needed embrace. Tension from the day's events lifted from her shoulders when she looked into his warm chestnut eyes, swimming with adoration. She hated herself for needing him. He was facing serious charges. He could be sent away for a handful of years. What if it was for an entire decade? How would she survive? Her throat tightened with the notion.

"Lucky for me, *your friends* aren't going out of their way to avoid my calls," he whispered in her ear, sounding both slightly amused and irritated. "I'm here for you, B. Whatever you need."

Kiersten stole her away for a tight embrace. "Don't hate me," she begged in Bexley's ear. "He was crazy worried when he couldn't get ahold of you. Now's not the time to push away the people you love."

Luke stepped in to hug her next. She half expected him to throw more gasoline on the fire, but he merely offered his condolences. As much as it irritated her that her closest allies had been conspiring against her, she was also somewhat soothed by their blatant support.

They all settled around the hightop table, Brewer and Kiersten flanking her on either side as a waitress swooped in to take their drink orders.

Kiersten glanced at Bexley over her menu. "So did you visit the captain's place?"

Bexley snorted. "Sure did."

"And?" Kiersten rolled a hand between them.

"And…I'm not going back without a hazmat suit and a bullet proof vest."

"What's that about?" Brewer demanded from her other side.

Letting out a long breath, Bexley turned to him. "When Cin and I went to the old man's house today, we discovered he'd moved out months ago. So Red tracked down an apartment he was renting." She let her shoulders drop. "I can't even begin to describe the place without using the words 'shit' or 'hole'. It's hard to believe anything lived there that didn't have four legs and a tail."

Brewer scratched his head. "Are you sure that's where he was living?"

"Red's good at her job—maybe even the best in the biz. I don't know how she got her hands on the rental agreement, but it looked legit. He'd signed it back in October."

"I cannot believe the captain was living a double life," Kiersten commented wryly. "You have no idea what was going on with him?"

"No, but I intend to find out."

"I can contact the probate court to see if a Will was filed," Luke offered. "If he appointed an executor outside of the family, they'd contact you about his Will eventually."

"That would be helpful," Bexley agreed, offering him a smile. "Thanks, Luke."

Kiersten wrapped her freshly-manicured fingers around Bexley's wrist. "And how about I arrange for a meeting between you and Cineste? I can act as a moderator, or whatever. You guys are way too close not to rise above your differences."

"You're fighting with your sister?" Brewer grumbled. "What's going on with you, Squires?"

"It's nothing I can't handle," Bexley assured them, pulling her arm from Kiersten's grip. "I'll smooth things out with her tomorrow. She just needs time to accept the fact that her dear old dad wasn't the superhero she imagined."

The waitress reappeared with their drinks, and started taking their orders.

Brewer nudged his shoulder against Bexley's. "Want me to tag along back to that apartment building?"

She pressed her lips together while weighing her options. She couldn't deny how much she favored the idea of returning with someone who'd had weapons and combat training in the military. Then again, she was afraid of what would happen if the judge on Brewer's case caught wind of him getting mixed up in trouble of any kind.

"I should be done with my last appointment tomorrow by two," he added. "Then I'm all yours."

Annoyed when her stupid heart squeezed, she sighed. He really was hers, in every way imaginable. Why was she so eager to put distance between them? Shouldn't she be enjoying what time they had left together?

"Maybe…" she conceded. "I'll let you know."

Once they'd placed their orders, the conversation switched from doom and gloom to lighter subjects that had them all laughing long after they were finished with their meals. Kiersten surprised everyone at the table by paying for their bill, then lifting what was left of her drink for a toast. Amused, Bexley and the men raised their nearly empty glasses along with her.

"Here's to the kind of friends who are more like family, and the hot boyfriends who put up with our shit." She turned to Luke with the biggest smile Bexley had ever seen. "Especially hot boyfriends who'd make an especially hot Mayor."

Bexley lowered her glass, blinking heavily. "Come again?"

Luke playfully hooked an arm around Kiersten's neck. "Guess the cat's out of the bag." He ran his other hand over his jet black hair, cheeks turning a dark crimson. "Someone has to try to straighten this city out. Figured I'd give it a try."

"That's—" Bexley began, dumbfounded. Although she'd come to rely on his legal expertise whenever she ran into trouble, she agreed that

Papaya Springs needed an ethical leader. She settled on saying, "Pretty awesome. Congratulations, Luke."

"I haven't won yet. The special election isn't until April."

"Wouldn't he make an awesome Mayor, though?" Kiersten gloated at his side.

Luke winked back at her. "And you'd make a pretty excellent mayoress."

When they held each other's gazes, smiling like love-struck fools, Bexley was hit with an ugly bolt of envy. There was nothing standing in their way of a happy future.

Bexley pushed away from the table. She looped her handbag over her head while clearing her throat. "Thanks again for dinner."

"I'll let you know sometime tomorrow whether or not I'm able to find anything on your dad," Luke told her, standing to pull Kiersten's chair back. "I'm in court all morning, but I should be able to look into it after lunch."

Despite the teasing smile on her glossy lips, Kiersten's eyes narrowed on Bexley. "Please do us all a favor, and talk to your sister. As soon as possible. I won't tolerate you two giving each other the cold shoulder at the service."

After Kiersten and Luke started for the parking lot, hand-in-hand, Brewer moved to Bexley's side. "That was…unexpected."

"It makes sense. This town needs someone honest to flip this corrupt city on its head."

The air crackled with electricity when Brewer's gaze held hers, and his lips twitched with a smirk. "Wanna come back to my place?"

Unable to fight the urge to touch him any longer, Bexley stood on her toes to wrap her arms around his neck. "I have to meet with someone," she confessed. "It shouldn't take too long. I'll meet you back at my apartment."

Locking his arms around her waist, he lifted a thick brow. "A lead on the mob princess's case?"

With a wry smile, she shook her head. "Thought I'd take that kid you chased away up on his offer." When he frowned, she dipped her chin and giggled. "I'll tell you everything later. I promise." Despite her growing reservations over their relationship, she kissed him long and hard. Truth be told, her heart longed for him to stay by her side while she talked to the witness, even though she sensed it was something she needed to do on her own.

Brewer grunted, cupping the back of her head

with a large hand and deepening the kiss more than Bexley deemed appropriate in public. Yet she was unable to resist, or ask him to stop. Her insides turned to jelly with every brush of his demanding lips and the scorching heat of his body. Oh, how she'd miss those intimate moments.

Brewer backed away with a twinkle in his eye and an insidious smirk on his beautiful mouth. "See if that kid can top *that*."

She watched him strut away, admiring the firm muscles and generous curves of his backside. Though the connection they shared went far beyond the physical realm, it didn't hurt that she was attracted to him like bees to honey laced with crack. The rush of heat she'd felt the night of their reunion was back with a vengeance, accompanied by a dizzying swarm of something in her belly.

*Damn that gorgeous man to hell and back,* she thought. She was sure the odd sensation squeezing her heart was love. And he was leaving her for a long while. Were there support groups for women with broken hearts?

Once he was out of sight, she made her way to a cluster of hostesses just inside the restaurant's entrance. "Excuse me. Can you tell me where I can find Christine Woodland?"

"Bexley?" A short woman with an angular face and a chic blond mane stepped out to greet her with a thin smile. "Let's go somewhere I can hear myself think."

Bexley followed Christine through the swarm of giddy patrons and beyond the building to the employee parking lot. With trembling fingers, the woman pulled a vape pen from her back pocket. "Once again, I'm sorry about your dad," she said, stopping to suck on the pen. "But I don't know what else I can tell you about that night." She tilted her head up to the twinkling stars and released a long stream of cotton candy scented smoke. "I was heading back from a friend's bachelorette party. I hadn't been drinking, because it's really not my thing and I had to work early the next morning. I was so tired that I almost took my friend up on the offer to crash at her place since my mom had the kids for the night. Then I decided that I wanted to be there when my kids woke in the morning."

"So you were driving on the same road?"

Taking another inhale, Christine nodded.

"Walk me through what you saw that night."

"It was dark. I didn't really see anything at first because I was on my phone," she admitted with reddening cheeks. "The road was basically empty and I was getting a little sleepy, so I was searching for my hard rock playlist. I looked up when I heard a blaring horn."

"Someone was honking at you?" Bexley assumed.

"No, it came from somewhere ahead of me. The Benz—um…your dad—was honking at the jerk who hit him. The accident happened so fast after that. I barely—"

"Hold on." Color draining from her face, Bexley held up a hand. "Back up a minute. You're saying he ran off the road because someone hit him?"

"Yeah." The girl's eyes narrowed. "I thought you said you already saw the report."

"I did. The report stated it was a single-vehicle accident. They said the tire marks indicated he hadn't swerved." Bexley snagged her phone from her handbag and retrieved the picture she'd scanned of the police report. "Take a look for yourself."

Christine squinted down at the screen, enlarging it with her fingertips. "I don't understand. That's not what I told them…I swear. The officer that did my interview made me repeat my statement over and over. He kept asking all these weird questions, making it sound like he doubted what I really saw. He tried to get me to confess that I was drunk, or that I had taken something. He didn't seem to believe a word I said."

"Did you get a good look at the other vehicle? The one who ran my father off the road?"

"Not really. It was going so fast that I hardly saw it before I realized the Benz was going to crash. It was an older, four-door car…black…with blackout windows."

"Did you notice anything else? Like did it have California plates?"

"No, I'm sorry. Like I said, it happened in the blink of an eye. I was so freaked out by the crash that I slammed on my breaks and just watched it happen." She handed Bexley's phone back, frowning. "Why would he change my statement?"

*Because someone has something important to hide,* Bexley decided.

All at once feeling a little faint, she passed a business card to Christine. "Please give me a call if you can remember anything else."

Christine called out a reply, but Bexley was too focused on dialing the number of the officer who had reported the incident to make out the girl's words. The officer's phone rang straight through to voicemail. "This is Officer Terrance Hill. I will be on personal leave until January tenth. If this is an emergency, please hang up and dial nine—"

Bexley ended the call. She hardly registered the fact that she'd found her way into her SUV, and was already on the busy highway that led to her apartment.

Cold fear clenched her jaw and trickled down her back. She was weighted down with the unshakable hunch that her father, the man with whom she'd felt indifferent about for years, had been murdered.

# CHAPTER SIX

True to his word, Brewer had chilled a bottle of Prosecco on ice in anticipation of Bexley's arrival home. Upon discovering he'd also drawn her a warm bubble bath and intended to give her a massage while she soaked, Bexley broke down in tears.

His strong arms slipped around her, carrying her to the couch where she had her first proper cry since learning of her father's death. She'd been so cold and heartless, even the slightest bit relieved when she first learned that he'd died. She let the tangled web of feelings for her father flow, soaking Brewer's t-shirt in the process. He silently stroked a hand over her head as she sobbed, and bent every few minutes to kiss the top of her head.

She eventually gave into the persistent pull of exhaustion, and let the reassuring beat of Brewer's heart lull her to sleep.

———

BEXLEY WOKE WITH A START. SHE WAS TUCKED IN her bed, and daylight spilled into the room. She bolted upright, gasping. Had she missed her chance to speak with the woman in the cafe?

"Bad dream?" Brewer asked in a scratchy voice.

Finding her phone charging on the nightstand at her side, she grabbed it to check the time. It was only a few minutes after midnight. She glanced toward the hallway, letting out a breath. The "daylight" was coming from the light in the hallway. "I thought I'd slept in too late."

"You've only been sleeping a few hours." Brewer tugged lightly on her arm. "Come on. You're exhausted."

She gave in, tossing her phone aside and falling into his arms. Then she looked down at the cotton material draping her body, and snorted. "How weird. I seem to be wearing your shirt again."

"It's not my fault you do weird stuff in your sleep. You should really see someone about that."

With a deliciously deep chuckle, he turned on his side to trap her in a protective bear hug. "Wanna tell me what set you off?"

With a shaky inhale, she repeated her conversation with Christine, and relayed her greatest fear of what the cover up could mean. Brewer absentmindedly traced his fingers across her shoulder between them as she spoke.

"What if I'm right, Hawk? What if someone killed him on purpose, and tried to cover their tracks?"

"Then you'll find them, have 'em brought to justice for your old man." The way he said the words with total confidence began to chip away at her doubts.

"Was I too hard on him?" she whispered. "Should I have forgiven him for all those years of disloyalty and neglect to us and my mom, and moved on the way he wanted?"

"Now's not the time to be hard on yourself, B." He pressed his forehead against hers, and sighed. "The resentment you felt toward him wasn't going to just disappear the day he decided to take it easy on you and your sister. The man had no clue how lucky he was to have you and Cineste as his daughters. I got the feeling he was a man with too many regrets to count. Maybe finding out he'd fathered another daughter is what finally sobered him up, made him realize he needed to do better."

"Oh my god," Bexley gasped, staring up at the ceiling fan. "I totally forgot about Sadie. She probably—I mean *I guess*—she deserves to know that he's gone."

"Do you know how to get in touch with her?"

"I wouldn't even know where to begin," she admitted with a wave of guilt.

"Maybe we'll find her contact info in his apartment."

"Kiersten was right." She wiggled out of his arms to search for her phone. "I need to call Cineste and make things right."

"You can call her in the morning."

"You don't understand. We can't go on like this. She's all I have left."

He maneuvered them both around until she was trapped beneath him, boxed in by his brawny arms, and frozen in place by the heat of his lust-driven stare. Her chest heaved with slow, labored breaths as he leaned down, pressing his soft lips to hers. He pulled back, dimple flashing with a grin, but his chestnut eyes remained stoic. "No, B. She's not all you have left."

Gawd, he was so very beautiful that her chest ached, making it hard to breathe.

And he was also so very wrong. All too soon he'd be gone.

———

At 6:03 a.m. Bexley strode into 770 Fix with a spring in her step and a spark in her eye. Brewer had given her a send-off she wouldn't forget as long as she breathed air, and she'd caught Cineste on her way to the gym. The sisters had a tearful reunion in which they both promised not to let their emotions come between them again. Bexley filled Cineste in on the latest about where their father had been living, and the suspected coverup after his accident. They made plans to meet up again once Brewer and Bexley had a chance to sort through the Captain's things.

While taking the smallest cup of coffee available from Rachel, Bexley's pulse skipped as a beautiful woman in a navy power suit entered the cafe. She perfectly matched the barista's description. Rachel caught Bexley's gaze with both eyebrows lifted and a slight nod.

Once the woman had placed her order, Bexley

placed herself directly in her path. She braced herself for the impact of the woman's elbow against her back, pleased when the contents of Bexley's loosely held handbag—most notably the enlarged photograph of "Brad"—scattered across the floor. Bexley wasn't as excited when her overpriced, scalding cup of joe followed, splashing against her jeans. Pain shot through her shins.

"Hhh—ottt!" she roared, dancing around.

The woman reached out to her, gasping. "Oh shit! I'm *so* sorry! I'm such a klutz! Are you okay?"

Still unable to catch her breath, Bexley grimaced.

Rachel came rushing around the countertop with a handful of towels.

"Don't touch her!" the other woman warned. "She needs to remove her jeans!"

"Oh, right!" Rachel said. She hooked a hand under Bexley's arm. "You can take them off in the back while I fill a bucket with cold water."

Bexley hobbled alongside Rachel. As they rounded the counter, Bexley spotted the slender woman crouched down over the floor, collecting Bexley's belongings. Her lips parted with a silent gasp when she spotted the picture of "Brad." There was no mistaking the recognition in her expression.

As mortifying as it was to strip down to her underwear in front of the teenager, Bexley was relieved to peel away the wet fabric to discover her legs were merely irritated, and not visibly burned. Rachel suggested they run cold water over them as a precaution.

The woman joined them, her expression tight with worry. She was elegantly beautiful, with round eyes in the darkest shade of brown imaginable, sharp cheekbones, and smooth dark hair down to the middle of her back. The material and cut of her suit was both fashionable and commanded respect. Her overall aura was so fierce that a Beyonce tune played in Bexley's head.

"How's it looking?" the woman asked.

"I needed a tan anyway," Bexley answered.

"Once again, I'm so, *so* sorry I burned you," the woman said, placing her hands over her heart. "I was up late last night working on a case. I'm not quite myself this morning." She then dug inside her purse and handed Rachel a $50 bill. "Please make her a new cup—make it a grande. And whatever else she wants off the menu."

"Just the coffee," Bexley told Rachel. With water still trickling down her shins, Bexley glanced at the woman. "Don't worry, I'm not sue happy or anything. It's my fault for not paying better attention."

"I have to admit, the idea of a lawsuit did cross my mind. The paranoia probably comes with being a corporate attorney." The woman laughed nervously, offering her hand. "Faye Odgren."

"Cineste Ferguson," Bexley replied, having been caught off guard. She was, after all, naked from the waist down aside from a swatch of lace underwear. And she had assumed the picture of the target would naturally start up a conversation—only she wasn't totally sure which direction it would go.

Faye pointed to Bexley's handbag on a stainless steel counter. "I dried off your things and put them back inside. Unfortunately, I think your picture got ruined."

Bexley feigned naivety. "My picture?"

Crossing over to the bag, Faye removed the 8x10 headshot and held it out between them. Her hand slightly trembled. "Are you a talent agent?"

"Oh that. Good looking, right?" Bexley paused, gauging the woman's reaction. "Too bad he's a total creep. I met him on a dating site, and the jerk later took some of my things."

Faye's slender fingers wrapped around her neck as her eyes became empty. "Oh?"

"I'd met him here once, so I've been bringing his picture with me, hoping someone recognizes him. He stole my grandmother's ring."

"How awful," Faye breathed out.

Bexley met her gaze. "Do you recognize him?"

"I'm sorry, I don't." The woman's eyes drifted past Bexley. "Have you filed a police report?"

"They said a stolen ring is low on their priority list." Bexley tried to hand the picture back. "Are you sure he doesn't look familiar?"

Faye's dark eyes dilated. "If I knew who he was, I'd turn him into the police for you."

That's when Bexley spotted the princess cut diamond of several carats on Faye's left ring finger. It explained her denial despite having an obvious association with the man in the picture. For one reason or another, it seemed reasonable to assume Faye had stepped out on her fiancé with "Brad."

"That ring wasn't worth much, but it was all I had left of my grandmother," Bexley muttered, attempting to rouse a few tears. "My parents died when I was little, so she raised me as her own. She passed away just last year. If I don't get it back, I'll be heartbroken."

Faye starred at the back exit, tight-lipped, and shifted her stance. Bexley could practically hear the wheels in her head turning. She clearly felt bad for Bexley, and was conflicted on whether or not it was worth exposing herself. "Do you have an extra picture of this dirtbag? This is my neighborhood. I could ask around...see if anyone in the area might know who he is."

"Go ahead and take that one," Bexley said, forcing it back into Faye's grip. "I can print out more at home. I'll give you my number in case you come up with anything."

With any luck, Faye's empathy would overturn the need to keep her reason for denying her involvement a secret.

SETTLED AT HER DESK IN A FRESH PAIR OF JEANS from home, Bexley read through the correspondence between Elizabeth and "Brad" once again. She kept hoping something about their conversation would jump out at her, providing a new lead. The only thing it provided was a reason to be glad she'd found Brewer the old fashioned way, and that she hadn't been subjected to a cheesy romance fueled by false promises, or hadn't taken part in conversations that could've been seen by anyone with basic knowledge of Red's hacking skills.

For the remainder of the morning, she drudged through smaller cases that required her attention. Though it was hard to focus on anything that didn't involve her father's fate or a $100k payout, and she'd become cynical enough to believe literally everyone in Papaya Springs was involved in an extramarital affair, there were still countless bills that needed to be paid.

As her empty stomach alerted her to the fact that it was nearing lunchtime, a message from Red popped onto her 49" monitor, providing a user name and passwords for three dating websites "Brad" had frequented. Bexley logged in to one of the sites, biting down on a giggle. Red had showcased her mad editing skills by transforming Bexley into a fair-skinned blonde with a larger chest and a nest of diamonds hanging around her neck. "Gweneviere Olsen," a successful influencer with millions of followers, almost could've passed for Elizabeth Ricci's older sister.

"Now that's one sexy woman," Brewer commented, suddenly inside her office. "Why do I get the feeling I've met *Gweneviere* before?"

The mouth-watering smell of barbecued ribs wafted through the stale office air before she turned to watch as he deposited a greasy bag on the edge of her desk. Although there was a faint smile on his lips, Bexley saw a brief sliver of hurt in his expression when he side-eyed her curved screen.

She lowered her chin and grimaced. "Would it sound too cliché to swear it isn't what you think?"

Looking completely unfazed, he sunk into the chair across from her with one shoulder lifted. "I wouldn't be committed to making this thing with you work if I didn't think you were completely honest with me."

Guilt nagged at her conscience. She hadn't been honest with him about so many other things. "I'm trying to bait a con man who targets wealthy women on dating sites."

"You'll have to let me know if you ever plan to meet up with this low-life in person." A wry smirk tugged at his lips. "I can loan you the perfect car to really sell *Gwen's* social status."

She huffed out a quiet laugh while distributing their usual orders from Rib King. Sometimes she was truly convinced Brewer Hawkins was too good of a thing—even more so when he started sucking barbecue sauce from his fingers with a twinkle in his eye.

"By the way, I'm all yours for the rest of the day," he told her. "My last appointment canceled."

"Perfect. I'll let the super at the captain's place know we're coming early."

Right as she retrieved her phone to make the call, it rang with a call from Luke. She turned away from Brewer as she answered, "Hey, Luke. Any luck?"

"Nothing has been filed with the probate court. If he did appoint an executor, they have thirty days to file after his death. I asked the clerk to notify me if anything comes in."

Disappointed, Bexley quietly sighed. "Thanks for looking into it."

"Hold on, Bex. There's more. I'm sorry to be the bearer of bad news, but in addition to your father's divorce, the clerk came across another recent file—a civil case."

"What kind of civil case?"

"Hillary was suing him in a proceeding separate from the divorce. The court wasn't going to award her anything because he'd filed for bankruptcy, but she believed he was hiding money elsewhere."

*Bankruptcy?* That would explain his living conditions, and maybe even his reason for stealing a car. But where had all his money gone? "You said the court *wasn't* going to award her anything. Does that mean the divorce wasn't final?"

"No, it wasn't. The judge assigned to their case had yet to issue a decree."

Eyes closed, Bexley leaned back into her office chair. "What happens to whatever is left of my father's estate if no one comes forward with a Will?"

"Because he filed for bankruptcy, there won't be anything left of his estate. At least not on paper. Whatever you find in that apartment he was renting is most likely all he possessed at the time of his death."

"What about his military benefits?"

An awkward pause followed. "Estate law isn't my specialty. You should contact the Navy."

"Give me your best guess."

Luke huffed out a long breath. "If your father's marriage to Hillary was still valid, and he hadn't filed anything to the contrary, I *believe* whatever pension and life insurance he had in place would be divided between his children and spouse."

*Hello, motive.*

Bexley pressed her fingertips to her eyelids. If her hunch was right and her father had been murdered, Hillary had just become the prime suspect.

## CHAPTER SEVEN

Witnessing the captain's decline in standard of living was almost enough to break Bexley. The only furnishings of his one-bedroom Eastside apartment included a soiled mattress without a box spring, and a broken recliner that was likely a freebie he'd found alongside the road. The worn, shaggy carpet stunk of mildew and urine. Less than half of the doors and dials on the ancient appliances in the compact kitchen were in working order. The toilet ran constantly, even after they'd tried yanking on the chain, and cockroaches scattered when they opened the mildew-stained shower curtain. When the super had met them with a set of keys, they discovered the door wouldn't latch shut.

It had taken a mere nudge of the portly man's boot to gain access.

While Brewer removed carpet staples and knocked on every square inch of the paneled walls in search of hidden compartments, Bexley silently rummaged through the unopened moving boxes piled on the bedroom floor. With her heart in her throat and her breath held, she carefully inspected each item she came across as if it had the ability to explode. It wouldn't have taken much at that point to tip her over the edge. Her father had become a virtual stranger with every discovery she'd already made.

"The only thing I found appeared to be the skeletal remains of an animal," Brewer reported as he shuffled into the room. He removed his leather gloves and stuck them under his arm. "If he was hiding money, it wasn't here. I think he was too smart to have done it somewhere this obvious anyway—especially when the front door wouldn't lock. You havin' any luck?"

Bexley kneaded the back of her sore neck. Glancing to the darkness outside the window, she realized they'd been at it for hours. "He didn't keep much of anything. I haven't even come across his medals." There also weren't any pictures of his family. She motioned to a box she'd set on the mattress. "It'll take days to sort through all the papers he kept."

"I'll help." Brewer tossed the gloves on top of the box and sat down beside her. After nudging her hand aside, he began to massage her tense muscles. "Maybe he rented a storage unit somewhere."

"Red already scoured the internet for anything secured under his name. If he was trying to hide something, he wouldn't have used his real name." She dropped her head forward as Brewer's fingers worked their magic. "What happened to make him live like this, Hawk?"

"I wish I knew, because I hate seeing you this way." He moved around, positioning her between his legs, and started using both of his hands to work on her knots. "Maybe it's time you pay Hillary a visit. Chances are pretty good she won't be happy to see you, but she might know something helpful— something that could shed a little light onto his situation."

Her lips twitched with a wry, tired smile. "While I'm at it, maybe I can ask if she ran him off the road."

"I know you don't like her, but do you think she's capable of murder?"

Bexley relaxed her shoulders as she considered his question. Hillary had no qualms committing adultery and falsely claiming she was assaulted in order to cover the fact that she was sleeping with someone who had more STDs than brain cells. It was possible she didn't possess *any* morals. "The only thing I'm sure of at this point? Those talented hands of yours could cure cancer. For a hot minute I almost forgot I'm camped out in this dump."

His lips fluttered over the nape of her neck, sizzling her nerve endings. "Let's grab those papers and blow outta here. We'll stop for champagne and strawberries on the way to your place."

With a tilt of her head, she frowned. "Strawberries and champagne?"

He gathered her in his arms, grinning in a way that stopped her heart. "I have big plans on how to bring in the new year with *Gweneviere*."

Her stomach plummeted. She'd ignored the fact that it was New Year's Eve. The prior year, she'd been foolishly duped by Dean Halliwell with a little romance before she exposed the fact that he was a serial killer. It wasn't something she cared to remember. And what if Brewer wasn't around for several New Years to come? Celebrating with him would only make for a more painful reminder of what was about to be taken away. It wasn't a holiday she intended to commemorate ever again.

She wiggled away to stand. "I'm not sure how long it'll take with Hillary."

"You're going to see her *tonight*?" He scrambled to his feet and shook his head. "B, ninety percent of Papaya Springs will be partying at the Royal. One of the guys at my shop said they hired some famous idiot from YouTube to deejay."

"Even better if I can catch her off guard."

He stepped closer, eyebrows lifted. "Want company?"

"You need a shower." She braced a hand on his chest. "Go home without me." Scooping up the box of papers, she started for the door. "I'll give you a call if it looks like I'll be back in time."

BEFORE RED CLOCKED OUT OF STRONGHOLD Investigations for the day, she was able to track down Hillary's current address. Bexley knocked on the door of the little bungalow half a dozen blocks from the beach, wondering how Hillary could afford the place if she hadn't received anything from the captain.

Her question was answered when the door was opened by the attractive 20-something man who had once hit on Bexley while serving her drinks at the PS Royal. Hillary's boy-toy wore a pair of low-slung gym shorts, and his impressive six-pack glistened with sweat.

"This is an unpleasant and undeniably awkward surprise," Bexley said, her tone flat.

"Oh look, it's Hillary's step-*sister*," Gage grumbled through gritted teeth.

"Says the same person who claimed not to know her an hour before he stuck his tongue down her throat." She tried to peer around him. "Is your mistress in, or is she out getting antibiotics?"

Based on the way he casually shrugged, she guessed the dig went sailing right over his dense head. "She's in the shower, getting ready. Whatever you want from her, I can tell you now that she's not interested."

A flash of the conversation Bexley had with Gage's ex in Denver came to mind. *He's too stupid to understand...*

"Getting ready?" she asked, feigning excitement. "Are you guys headed to the bash at the Royal? I hear they're having a celebrity deejay. Should be a *killer* party."

"As a matter of fact, we are." As if understanding his mistake, his expression leveled as he ran a hand over his wild dark hair styled in a faux hawk. "But you have to have an invitation to get in, and I *know* my boss wouldn't have extended one to a sleazy *investigator*." His deep dimples appeared with a mocking smile as he began to shut the door. "Have a nice life."

Grinning to herself, Bexley returned to her SUV, waving when she noticed Gage watching through a window. She dialed the one person on her contact list who undoubtedly could help. "I have a favor to ask…"

AS SOMEONE WITH A FINGER ON THE PULSE OF THE fashion and entertainment industries, Kiersten was immediately in awe of the attendees as she stepped into the Royal ballroom at Bexley's side several hours later. The disgustingly rich and über-famous mingled in tuxedos and sparkling dresses, crystal flutes in hand. Strobe lights flickered from above to the beat of a catchy pop tune. Bexley herself was impressed by how many familiar faces she'd seen on billboards and the big screen. It was clearly the who's who event of Papaya Springs.

In a bronze sequined cocktail dress, blond hair woven in complicated braids at the nape of her neck, Kiersten was as beautifully put together as the A-list actress who nudged her way past them. With a muffled squeal, Kiersten clutched Bexley's arm. "I can't believe Temperance got us in! We're totally having roses and champagne delivered to her tomorrow!"

"Don't get your designer undies in a twist," Bexley grumbled. "With any luck, we'll find Hillary right away and this won't take long. Besides, your *real* date is waiting for you, Cinderella."

Luke had been surprisingly graceful when Bexley asked to borrow his girlfriend for a couple of hours, even telling them to take their time and enjoy the party.

"Regardless," Kiersten said, sizing up the white pantsuit she'd sent Bexley for their class reunion, "I'm glad you had another excuse to wear that. Everyone's going to think you're an up-and-coming model. Mark my words."

A snort burst from Bexley's lips. "Let's get this over with before security learns you're certifiable and ejects you from the party." She pointed to the left of the grand ballroom decorated in high quality silver, gold, and black streamers and balloons. "You cover that side, and I'll sweep the area on the other side, ending with the deejay booth. Meet me back here in twenty minutes. If you see Hillary before then, text me."

With a wicked grin, Kiersten rubbed her hands together. "Oooo...I love it whenever I get to play your sidekick. I feel like I'm in one of those murder-mystery movies!"

Seconds after they parted ways, an attractive waiter handed Bexley a flute of champagne. She took a sip, acknowledging the wealthy knew how to party as the fantastically sweet liquid slid down to her stomach. She took her time perusing the crowd, doing her best to pretend she belonged among them despite the contradiction of her minuscule bank account balance. She was halfway through the grand room when she heard the familiar Spanish trill of a voice calling, "Miss Bexley!"

Temperance Rose made her way through a group of men and women with a bright, friendly smile aimed in Bexley's direction. It would never *not* shock Bexley that she'd formed a bond with the sultry reality star, and that Temperance considered her a good friend. In a metallic blush mini dress, dark hair a mass of seductive curls that artfully highlighted her large chest, makeup professionally applied in a way that made her big brown eyes and bronze skin glow more than usual, Temperance projected sheer radiance.

Taking Bexley's hands in hers, Temperance air-kissed each of her cheeks. "You made it! And you look *preciosa*!"

"I can't thank you enough for getting us in last minute," Bexley said, squeezing the woman's petite hands. "You look stunning as always."

As if she materialized out of thin air, Bexley's newest client was suddenly standing among them. Elizabeth wore a knee-length, scarlet red dress with a high slit, twin spaghetti straps covering one shoulder, ears dripping with diamonds. Every man within throwing distance was going out of their way to stare at the blonde siren, tongues practically wagging.

"Who would've guessed you clean up so well?" Elizabeth said to Bexley, smirking. "I had to look twice to make sure it was really you."

"It's...really me," Bexley answered smartly.

Elizabeth jutted one hip, frowning. "What's the status on my case?"

Bexley briefly glanced at Temperance. "Why

don't you come by my office tomorrow so we can discuss it in private?"

"Temp knows everything." Elizabeth paused, rolling her eyes. "Well, almost everything."

"It's still a little early to say, but I'm working a lead," Bexley answered cryptically. "Once I have information of value to pass along, I'll be in touch."

Temperance nudged Elizabeth with her shoulder. "I told you Miss Bexley is *increíble*, no?"

"That has yet to be seen." Elizabeth pressed her svelte lips together and scanned the crowd with an appreciative expression. "Ladies, you'll have to excuse me from this dull conversation. There's a room full of beautiful men waiting to be seduced." She slinked away, blowing kisses at a group of men.

"I have to get going as well," Bexley told Temperance. "Thanks again for getting me in last minute. One of these days I'll find a way to repay you for everything."

"You work too much, Miss Bexley," Temperance scolded. "You must take more time to enjoy life." Then her face broke into a brilliant smile. "There will come a time when I will whisk you away on my jet to somewhere beautiful so you can relax and enjoy your handsome *amante*."

Bexley shook her head, confused. "My hand-some what?"

Although Temperance had already walked away, a deep voice rattled in her ear, "It's Spanish for 'lover'."

Air whooshed from Bexley's lungs as she spun around, finding Brewer smirking down on her. In a navy blue suit. Hair slicked back. Putting every well-known actor and model Bexley had come across that night to shame.

"It's time we talk about what's going on here," he said.

It was so unfair that they didn't have more time together. If her father's death had taught her anything, it was that life was too short to tiptoe around hard feelings. For the second time that day, she felt as if a piece of her had broken. She was both crazy about Brewer, and on the verge of losing him. She clung to his strong arms, gazing meaning-fully into his glistening chestnut eyes.

"Hawk, I…ah, *really* don't know how to say this," she began. "I'm literally *the worst* at this kind of thing. I hope you realize by now that you mean a lot to me. More than I ever could've imagined myself caring for a man. But I think—"

With a pained expression, his lips sealed over

hers. Her lungs seized when the truth dawned on her: he thought she was breaking up with him. As if to confirm her fear, Brewer's arms locked around her, and their kiss deepened. Suddenly it was as if everyone in the room was applauding them. Then Brewer backed away, and she realized they were clapping for someone speaking in front of the ballroom.

She turned in that direction, standing on her tip toes for a better look. Luke stood on the stage, wearing a tuxedo, microphone in hand. "I'd like to ask my girlfriend to join me up here."

What was happening? Had Brewer and Luke crashed the party together?

Brewer wrapped Bexley's hand inside his, and pulled her toward the front of the ballroom. "Come on, you won't want to miss this."

# CHAPTER EIGHT

Kiersten slowly ascended the stage's steps, her wide eyes and frequent glances at the crowd making her appear as bewildered as Bexley felt. Luke greeted her with a hug and a chaste kiss before taking her hand and turning to address the crowd. "This stunning beauty has completed me in ways I never thought possible. I always figured I'd die a bachelor because I could never find anyone who could tolerate my ways. But she's made me both a better man, *and* a better dresser." He paused, grinning, as everyone laughed. "You think I'm kidding, but I assure you, I'm not. This woman knows fashion."

Bexley took a deep, stuttering breath when he knelt on one knee and presented Kiersten with a small box. "Kiersten Douglas, you're the love of my life, the spark of light that brightens my darkest days. Will you do me the honor of becoming my wife?"

Bexley stood frozen, mouth agape. She had sensed her best friend would be married before long, and she was ecstatic that Kiersten had found Luke. They were a perfect match. But she wasn't expecting to feel an ugly surge of envy once it happened. It wasn't like she wanted the commitments that came with marriage. The idea of having to share absolutely everything for the rest of her life and report to someone on a regular basis wasn't the least bit appealing.

Brewer squeezed her hand, and she met his questioning gaze. Maybe marriage wasn't as complicated as she thought. Her connection to Brewer had been relaxed from the beginning. Maybe a legal document wouldn't change anything. What if he was The One?

"Oh my god, *yes!*" Kiersten squealed from the stage. "Nothing could make me happier!"

Bexley's eyes slid back to her friend. Luke stood, and Kiersten launched herself into his arms for a kiss. The crowd roared with laugher when the deejay queued "Another One Bites the Dust."

While everyone was still facing the same direction, Bexley closely observed the party goers. Less than a few yards away, she suddenly spotted her reason for being there. It was unlikely Hillary was aware it was Bexley's best friend she was cheering for as she whooped it up from inside Gage's arms.

Bexley tugged on Brewer's suit sleeve, bringing his ear down to her mouth. "Showtime. Wish me luck." He responded with a simple nod, but his expression was wary.

As Bexley made her way through the crowd, Hillary's eyes all at once locked on her. At Hillary's side, Gage also spotted Bexley and scowled. The couple began a mad dash in the other direction.

"Hillary, wait!" Bexley called after them. She quickened her pace, shoving partygoers aside along the way. She wasn't going to give up easily. "I know there's no love lost between us, but this is important!"

Once the couple breached a more condensed crowd, Bexley lost sight of them. Assuming they were headed toward the exit, she dashed around to the far side and ran like her life depended on getting to them in time. She reached the ballroom's main entrance, and stood watch until she caught sight of Hillary's glittering headband. Once again, the two women locked gazes, and Hillary darted back in the other direction.

Bexley took a mad run at them. Convinced she'd lose sight of Hillary again, she dove through the air, landing on top of her squealing ex-step-mother. Many guests nearby gasped. Others scattered like terrorists were afoot. Several security guards materialized. One pointed a gun in Bexley's direction.

"Hands up where I can see them!" the burly man barked.

"Alright! Don't shoot!" Bexley conceded, rolling off Hillary and exposing the palms of her hands. Considering her history with New Year's Eve, it was par for the course. "Suppose you could do me a favor, and grab that lover-boy off the stage?"

---

IN A CAFE SEVERAL BLOCKS FROM THE ROYAL, Hillary sipped on a cappuccino across the little round table from Bexley. Her hair and makeup were destroyed, and one of the spaghetti straps on her silver cowl-neck dress had torn during the tackle. Bexley felt a touch of satisfaction knowing she'd wrecked the ridiculously young look Hillary had tried pulling off. Hillary may have been closer to Bexley's age than the captain's, but she had a good decade on Gage. Someone needed to remind her that she was nearing forty, and wasn't some 20-something coed.

"You're lucky they didn't throw your nosy ass in jail," Hillary growled with a deathly stare. "You managed to humiliate both of us in front of the most important people in Papaya Springs *and* Los Angeles combined."

"I have a feeling I'll still be able to sleep at night," Bexley said. When security had tried to haul her away in handcuffs, Temperance, Kiersten, Luke, and Brewer had all come running to her aid. Luke and Temperance had smooth-talked the head of security into releasing her, and Brewer had convinced Gage to take a walk with him so the two women could talk in private.

Sitting taller in the plastic chair, Bexley cleared her throat. "Are you ready to clue me in on what happened to my father's money?"

Hillary set the cup down, snorting. "Your guess is as good as mine. He did an excellent job hiding the fact that he was broke. I didn't notice anything until after our marriage started going south. I first suspected something when we received several calls at the house from collection agencies. Your father claimed it was a misunderstanding. I believed him until we received a notice of eviction."

"So you were *both* lying through your teeth at that point."

"I know you blame me for cheating on him, but your father had already distanced himself long before I met Gage. He would disappear for entire weekends at a time without bothering to tell me where he was going. When I finally confronted him about one of his mysterious trips, he said he'd gone fishing in Mexico with some friends. I knew he was lying, because I'd followed him out of town. He was headed north before I lost him. For all intents and purposes, our marriage was finished a long time ago. I started sleeping with Gage because I was lonely. Your father didn't seem to notice when *I'd* go missing for days at a time."

It seemed the captain had more going on than a simple affair. He'd invested in something that was depleting his cash flow. Bexley's mind wandered with the possibilities. *Drugs? Gambling? Prostitutes?* It was laughable that her mind immediately went to dark places when she was talking about her father. She couldn't remember him getting so much as a speeding ticket. "You still don't know where he was really going on those weekend trips?"

"I tried doing a little *investigation* of my own," Hillary explained with a scowl, "but he kept his credit card statements in a locked drawer. And when I tried following him again, he caught me."

"What makes you think he was hiding money?"

Hillary huffed and rolled her eyes, likely irritated that Bexley was privy to the details of her civil lawsuit. "No matter what was going on, he always had a stack of cash on him. After we lost the house, I witnessed him paying the movers and his bankruptcy attorney with a handful of hundred dollar bills."

"Who was his attorney?"

"Some guy named Kramer. I think your father found him in the phone book."

Bexley made a mental note to see what this "Kramer" guy could tell her. "If you truly believe he was hiding money, I'm going to assume you didn't see the pathetic excuse for an apartment he'd moved into after you lost the house. Suing him was a waste of your time and resources."

"That man was the master at keeping up appearances. After he'd filed for bankruptcy, he couldn't let anyone know that he had money." Leaning in closer, Hillary pressed her fingertips against Bexley's wrist. "Sweetheart, I'm going to give you a little 'motherly' advice. Whatever you may *think* you know about your father's situation at the time of his death, you're dead wrong. Let it go. Let *him* go. He's not worth *your* time."

While it was entirely possible the apartment had been a facade, Bexley had heard enough. Without another glance in Hillary's direction, she rose to her feet and started for the exit.

"Bexley?" She heard Hillary push away from the table. "You owe me a new dress!"

"Add it to your lawsuit!" Bexley scoffed over her shoulder.

As Brewer slept through the wee hours of the New Year in the next room, Bexley combed through the box of papers she'd taken from her father's sad little apartment. By no surprise, the captain had been a stickler about keeping receipts and tax documents from the past seven years. He'd continued to earn a healthy salary from the Navy up until the day he retired, and his expenses were modest. For a time, the biggest splurges were for salons and spas billed in Hillary's name.

Then she came across a stack of credit card charges on an account solely in the captain's name. She forced herself to start with the oldest records so she could track any changes in his spending habits. At first, there was nothing out of the ordinary. Then, just days after his retirement ceremony, there had been several thousand-dollar transfers to a bank account in Minnesota. Bexley racked her brain, trying to remember if her father had ever mentioned *anything* about the Midwest.

The next repeat charge was even more interesting. For almost the entire year leading up to his death, the captain's personal credit card reflected a weekly charge to "Two Pelicans Resort and Casino" in Oregon. The amount fluctuated, and was always accompanied by a sizable cash withdrawal from an ATM. With a quick estimation, he'd spent somewhere around $90,000 in ten months. It seemed her father *had* been into gambling after all. While it wasn't the explanation she'd been expecting, it also wasn't set in stone. He could have other reasons for staying at the casino.

"How long have you been up?" Brewer's groggy voice rumbled from the hallway.

"Not long," Bexley lied. She refused to turn around to face him, knowing his sleepy appearance would make her want to return to bed for a snuggle and whatever else they were in the mood for. Their conversation at the party hadn't been brought up again, and she wanted to keep it that way. If she exposed any more emotions, she was afraid she'd unravel the last thread of her sanity. "Have you heard of Two Pelicans Casino?"

"The one right over the Oregon border?" he asked. "A buddy in the service grew up in that area. His parents were both dealers there. Why?"

"Turns out the captain went there on a weekly basis for *months*."

"Your old man was a gambler?"

Feeling totally defeated, Bexley sank back into the cushions. "Not that I knew of, but he was already hiding an abundance of secrets. What's one more?"

Mussing his wild hair with one hand, Brewer sat on the couch at her side. He only wore a pair of tight boxer-briefs in her favorite shade of blue. "Might be worth a trip up there. If he was that frequent of a customer, someone's bound to remember him." He gently squeezed her thigh. "If you want some company—"

"You can't *leave* the *state*," she reminded him in a sharper tone than she intended. She was distracted by his natural scent and all that golden, tattooed skin covering rippling muscles. Facing her feelings for someone about to spend time in prison with violent offenders wasn't something she could handle. "I don't need you anyway."

He barked out a cold laugh. "Are you sure about that?"

Of course she wasn't sure. But she couldn't let him know that. He'd see her as being weak. Crossing her arms, she met his gaze. "You said you expected complete honesty from me, and there it is. I don't need you or anyone else to hold my hand. In fact, it might be better if you gave me space until I've had time to figure some things out."

"On that note, I'm going to head out." Holding his jaw tight, he stood. "I get that you're having a hard time with what happened to your father, B. What happened is messed up." His eyes hardened. "But as much as I've tried to be there for you and show my support, you're so hot and cold that I can't deal with it anymore. The push and pull is making me dizzy as hell. I'm not going to wait around until you decide to dump me while you're in one of your moods. Do us both a favor, and don't bother calling me until you're damn sure of exactly what you want from me."

Bexley's eyes prickled with tears as she watched him head back into the bedroom, presumably to grab his things. She knew exactly what she wanted and she couldn't have it, so she was pushing him away just as she'd done with Grayson. Though her reasoning this time around was different, Brewer deserved better. He'd given her the space she required, and hadn't asked for anything in return. She was starting to think it was in his best interest to wash his hands of her, and move on.

Blinking the moisture from her eyes, she pulled up the Two Pelicans Casino website on her phone to confirm they were open on the holiday. Since it was a ten hour drive and her father's service was in two days, she booked a flight, hotel, and rental car.

She'd just finished charging everything to her card when Brewer slipped out the front door, slamming it shut. She contemplated following him until her phone buzzed with a call from a blocked number.

"Bexley Squires."

"Hello, *Miss Squires*. I had a feeling the story about your grandmother's ring was a ruse to gain my sympathy, so I asked the barista what she knew about you." Faye huffed out a loud sigh, then clicked her tongue. "Once I found out who you really were, I thought about it long and hard. I decided if you're really an investigator, you must be after the guy in that picture for a good reason. Hopefully one that involves preventing other clueless women from being robbed blind."

"You're absolutely right, Ms. Odgren. He's scamming women on *multiple* sites. Someone has to stop him."

"Meet me at the Break-fast Surf Club in half an hour. I'll tell you everything I know about the lying son-of-a-bitch."

# CHAPTER NINE

In a baseball cap pulled down to her eyes—sleek dark ponytail poking through the hole in the back—black leggings and a long-sleeved wick away jogging top, Faye was nearly unrecognizable when she signaled to Bexley from a booth in the back corner of the bright and exceptionally clean cafe. Posters from popular 80s movies and vinyl records from the same era lined teal green walls. Neon pink chairs and stainless steel tables stretched out across a black and white checkered floor. It was an unusually warm day, and a heady ocean breeze swept through the building's open windows as Bexley continued past a handful of other patrons hunched over their morning brew of choice.

"Thanks for deciding to meet with me," she

said, taking a seat across from Faye and setting her handbag at her side.

Faye leaned over the table. "I'd appreciate it if you could keep what I'm about to tell you between the two of us. I've built a highly successful career, and I'm engaged to a really great guy. I don't want John or the professionals I work with thinking I'm in the habit of messing around."

Bexley nodded while digging for her phone. "I'll credit whatever you can tell me to a confidential source."

A waitress came by their booth and took Bexley's order of straight black coffee. Once the two women were alone again, Bexley gave Faye an encouraging smile. "Let's start at the beginning. Take your time."

Wetting her lips and taking a deep breath, Faye nodded several times like she was psyching herself up. "After John asked me to marry him, I had a moment of panic. He was a real ladies man while in the Marine Corp. His friends always joke about how he has a village of children overseas that he's never met." Faye's eyes drifted to the window, watching a group of surfers bobbing in the ocean on their boards. "I've only slept with one other guy in my entire life. I was afraid I might be making a mistake by committing myself without having more experience." Her watering eyes met Bexley's. "I wanted to see what else I might be missing, you know?"

Bexley couldn't imagine being in Faye's situation, but she nodded empathetically.

"I figured my secret was safe if I went through an anonymous hook up site. The guy you're looking for was so incredibly attractive that I couldn't believe he was interested in me. I was a little afraid that I was being cat-fished. He offered to meet me at the Seven-Seventy for coffee. I didn't tell him anything about myself, so I was floored that he'd suggested my favorite place. I was foolish enough to think it was a sign that we were meant to cross paths. Now that I've had time to think about it, I believe he was already following me around at that point. I swear he was tracking the GPS on my phone the way he was always one step ahead of me. Whenever we spoke, he just happened to be in the exact same neighborhood." Faye scrubbed both hands over her face. "Anyway, we met up for coffee, and things moved really quickly from there. We physically connected on a level that blew me away, and slept together three times in a week. I would get a room at the Royal, and he'd come up an hour after I checked in. After the last time, he said he wanted to get to know the real me better, and suggested we go to my place. By then I realized I'd made a mistake, and I was terrified that John would find out. The dude got angry…called me all sorts of awful names, and said he never wanted to see me again. The next night—the same day he'd suggested we meet at my place—my apartment was ransacked while I was sleeping. He took everything of value, including my original engagement ring. I took it off every night because it snagged my sheets."

Faye twisted the large diamond around her ring finger. "The worst part of all this was the way John was so sweet and understanding. He replaced my ring within twenty-four hours."

"You're not this guy's only victim," Bexley said, reaching out to touch the woman's hands. "I'm starting to suspect no one has reported him because they're too embarrassed to explain the circumstances to authorities."

Faye cringed. "Or they're afraid their significant others will find out."

"Do you remember any physical features that I could work with? Physical defects of any kind, tattoos, birthmarks…"

Faye set her chin in her hand, and tapped a finger against her cheek while she thought it over. "He had this little tattoo on his left shoulder. It was really faded, but it reminded me of the gang symbols I'd see spray painted on buildings when I was growing up in L.A. Aside from that, he was perfect. If he wasn't a con artist, he probably could make an honest living as an actor or model."

"This is all helpful, Faye." Bexley said while typing a few notes into her phone. "Is there anything he said or did that stood out to you as unusual?"

"I have a feeling he never stated a single fact that was even remotely close to the truth. Even though he claimed to have been born and raised in California, he had the slightest bit of a European accent. Maybe Italian. And he claimed he was an FBI agent when we first met, but in another conversation we talked about places we've visited, and he said he'd never been to Virginia. God, I can't believe I agreed to see him again after that. It was so obvious he was lying to impress me." She dropped her face into her hands. "Oh god, I'm such an idiot!"

She was far from it. She'd given Bexley a considerable amount of information in comparison to Elizabeth. "No use beating yourself up over it. The best thing you can do is give me a call if you remember anything else that could help me catch this lowlife." Bexley stood, looping her handbag around her head. "I'm sorry, but I have a plane to catch. You've already been *incredibly* helpful, Faye."

Eyes wide, Faye raised the palms of her hands. "Hold on a minute! I just remembered something!" She stood to face Bexley. "The last time we were together, I saw a call flash across his screen from Papaya Springs Facial. It's a clinic downtown that offers plastic surgery procedures. I pretended to be sleeping, because at that point I knew he was lying about everything, and I wanted to hear him being honest for a change. He apologized for missing his weekly facial, and asked them to reschedule. What kind of *man* gets a *weekly facial?*"

"One highly aware his looks are his sole asset in life?" Bexley's pulse raced. She had a solid lead that she could work with, so long as "Brad" kept up with his beauty regimen. "Do you remember what day it was when he asked to have the appointment rescheduled?"

"It was a Friday...I wanna say around nine, because we had...well, *you know*, after grabbing coffee at the cafe." Faye's eyes narrowed. "Promise me you're going to stop him from doing this again."

"I'll do my very best to hang him out to dry."

***

By early evening, Bexley was navigating the compact rental car from the airport in Southern Oregon to the casino. The area was breathtakingly beautiful. Snow-topped mountains, small streams, and grand pine trees lined the roads along her journey, winding toward a modern castle-like structure overlooking a wide valley dotted with houses and two-story businesses. TWO PELICANS RESORT & CASINO flashed in neon letters along the side of the newly constructed stone building. The parking lot was packed with vehicles, explaining the inflated price Bexley was forced to pay for one night. With a quick perusal of the town below, it appeared there wasn't much else for the locals to do on a holiday.

Bexley found a spot on the far end of the lot, and started for the building. For a blissful moment, she let herself pretend she could live a different life —one in which she owned a cabin in a sleepy little community such as that one, married to Brewer. Maybe they'd even have a couple of big dogs. She'd never seen Brewer hiking, but he'd mentioned it was a favorite pastime while in the service, and she could picture him decked out in hiking gear with a deep tan from countless hours of exploring the mountains at her side. She'd be happy doing nothing more than snuggling by the fireplace, dogs sleeping on her feet, drinking hot chocolate with her man…

Her phone rang, jerking her back to reality. Her heart sank when Cineste's picture filled her phone's screen. She'd forgotten about their meeting with the funeral director.

"Cin, I'm so sorry I forgot about—"

"Forget it. I know it's not your scene anyway. I have it under control. But what's this about you and Brewer taking *a break?*" Cineste roared. "I swear you're finally losing your *damn* mind!"

"Who says I had one to lose?" Bexley muttered. There was no point in arguing with her sister when she was fired up. "Can we talk about this later? I'm headed into the casino where *our father* secretly spent a lot of time and money behind his third wife's back."

Cineste continued to rant without acknowledging Bexley's situation. "I don't understand you. First you push Grayson away even though he was incredibly close to perfect for you, and now you're doing the same to Brewer who, by the way, literally checks every box of *every* woman's greatest fantasy, and somehow manages to bring out the very best in my commitment-phobic sister. Do you have an aversion to good men? Do you realize what you're throwing away?"

Irritation clenched Bexley's throat. Her little sister had *one* serious relationship, and she suddenly thought she was an expert. "First of all, *my relationships* aren't your business the same way I don't ride you about yours. How'd you find out, anyway?"

"When you didn't show at the funeral home and wouldn't answer your phone, I called Brewer. He was incredibly sweet as he explained the fact that you needed time to decide what you wanted from him. He said he wanted to be there to support our family, but the timing wasn't right for you. What *the hell*, Bex?"

"You've made your share of mistakes. Have I ever rubbed them in your face?"

"My situation with Alex was way different."

Something snapped, and Bexley's anger unfurled. "So is mine! The man I'm out-of-my-mind in love with is going to *prison*! Do you have any idea the kind of messed up thoughts that have been going through my head? Can you imagine worrying about whether or not your man is going to be attacked by violent offenders for god knows how long, and feeling selfish for wondering how many days you'll have to survive on your own without him? You haven't walked in my shoes, Cineste! I would *never* presume to know what it's like to walk in *yours*, so back off!"

"Whoa," Cineste said, her voice all at once calm and low. "Did you just say you're in *love* with him? Bex, that's…a monumental step for you. Have you told him yet? Does he know that you're freaked out about his time in prison?"

It was hard to breathe once Bexley realized she'd spilled the secrets she'd carefully guarded for months. A group of young adults breezed past, laughing and bouncing around like they were living their best lives. Why did it seem everyone around her had the ability to be happy without self-sabotage?

"I can't do this right now, Cineste."

"Tell Brewer everything you just said to me before it's too late. I care about you way too much to step back and watch as you destroy the best thing that's ever happened to you. I get that it's crappy timing, and you're not dealing so well with Dad's death, but don't let Brewer slip away because you're struggling with your emotions. I can tell he loves you too. Promise me you'll call him as soon as I hang up. Promise you won't blow this off, Bex."

The musical sounds of slot machines and the blinding glow of fluorescent lights overwhelmed Bexley as she waltzed in through the automatic doors. She'd never been interested in gambling, and had never taken the time to visit a casino, although she had a vague idea of what to expect from movies. "Yeah, okay," she finally told her sister. "I'll be in touch."

For three solid hours, Bexley questioned nearly every employee on the complex property, and gave them her business card. Whenever she was sure she'd covered every square inch of the place, she'd turn another corner and find a whole new section that felt endless. It was a windowless maze of bright colors and exciting sounds that both jarred Bexley from her self-deprecation, and made her question even more why a man who thrived on order was so drawn to something so chaotic.

Several of the casino's dealers recognized the captain, but they didn't know anything beyond the fact that they'd never witnessed him placing a bet. They all made the comment that he seemed to enjoy watching others gamble their money away. A bartender in his 70s told Bexley they'd had many conversations about their similar experiences while serving in the Navy, but the man didn't know anything about the captain's personal life, and said he always came alone.

Other than those weak leads, Bexley didn't have any more of an insight into the captain's secret life. Feeling both defeated and exhausted, she headed toward the front desk of the hotel. Her flight left before the sun would rise, and she needed to spend time deciding how she was going to handle the situation with Brewer.

Inside the hotel elevator that would take her up to her room on the sixteenth floor, she was joined by a curvy, light brown skinned woman with wavy dark hair and full red lips in cropped leggings with tennis shoes and a t-shirt, black smock draped over one arm. The woman gave Bexley a once-over. "You the one askin' everyone about the captain?"

"I am," Bexley confirmed, feeling a renewed jolt of energy. "Did you know him?"

"Of course I know him." The woman snapped her bubble gum and set a hand on her hip. "I remember first seeing him comin' around all those months ago when he started out as Kortney's regulars. Those two became like peas in a pod *real* fast."

"Her regular?" Bexley repeated, mentally crossing her fingers. *Please be anything other than a prostitute.*

"At the resort spa. She's one of the most popular masseuses."

Bexley hoped this Kortney wasn't the type that offered alternate endings with her services. "Is Kortney working today?"

"Nah…she's in Boise for the holidays, visiting family. I just got done covering her shift. She'll be back on Saturday though."

Bexley held her hand out between them. "Thank you for the information…"

Smiling, the woman shook Bexley's hand, pumping it with a firm grip. "It's Meli."

"I'd appreciate anything you could tell me about the captain." Bexley fished a business card out of her handbag, and passed it to Meli. "Are you and Kortney close?"

"We've been working together for five years. She's like my little sister." The woman studied the card, for a moment, then her narrowed gaze held Bexley's. "This you? You don't look like a PI."

"So I've heard."

"What do you want from Kortney? Is she in some kind of trouble?"

Bexley got the impression the woman was ready to warn her friend about Bexley for whatever reason, so she decided it was better not to divulge too much information. "I just have a few questions. It's nothing serious."

The elevator dinged, and the doors slid open. Bexley held the button to keep the doors open while turning back to the woman. "I'm curious, Meli. What did you mean when you mentioned Kortney and the captain were 'like peas in a pod'?"

"Please," Meli scoffed. "Anyone with a set of eyes can see it—those two are *crazy* about each other! I'm surprised they haven't run off to Vegas yet, and made it official! But based on the size of the rock she's wearin', I'm guessin' they have a big ol' ceremony planned."

# CHAPTER TEN

The raging thunderstorm perfectly suited Bexley's mood as she beat her fist against Brewer's motel door. She was soaked to the bone, and as angry as a wet hen. She didn't have the patience to wait for her flight home the next day, and had driven the rental through the night all the way from Oregon back to Southern California.

Part of her wanted to move on, and forget her father had ever existed. Another part wished he was still around so she could inform him of all the ways he'd failed his family while selfishly becoming absorbed in another life they'd been oblivious to.

The motel door flung open. In his favorite pair of gray sweat pants and no shirt, Brewer scowled back at her, his expression rigid. *Cold.* Bexley hated seeing him that way. She'd come to treasure the sparkle in his eye and the teasing grin that constantly played on his alluring lips. It took everything she had not to fling her arms around his neck and confess how badly she needed him.

"Thought you were in Oregon," he muttered, squaring his stance and tightening his jaw.

Rain streamed down Bexley's face. "I think I figured it out." She attempted to swallow the lump bobbing against her throat. "I think I know why I'm…*scared*…the reason I keep treating you in a horrible way you don't deserve."

Brewer's handsome features softened a little as he nudged the door all the way open. "Tell me about it inside. You're drenched."

With a shake of her head, she held her ground. "I've spent my entire life trying to separate myself from the captain…trying to prove to the world that I'm strong enough to survive anything and everything, despite the fact that my own father never believed in me." Raindrops camouflaged the tears that tumbled down her cheeks. "Deep down, I think I'm terrified it's in my DNA to end up just like him. I'm afraid I'll burn through marriage after marriage, never satisfied with what I have…that I'll never be able to appreciate the fact that I've found the perfect man—that I've found *you*. I was married for a hot minute in college because I was desperate for a different name—a fresh start. Until you came along, I didn't know what it was like to legitimately need someone…not because I can't take care of myself, but because I'm madly in love. And that scares the living hell out of me."

Brewer's lips finally twisted with his trademark grin. He took a step closer, eyes dancing with hope as he slid a hand over her side. "You're 'madly in love' with me, Squires?"

"Shhh…quiet!" she scolded, gently pushing him back with the palm of her hand. "You're going to make me lose my train of thought!" Her eyes rolled upward as she ran through the speech she'd perfected on the drive back. "I said the DNA thing…college…the part about loving you…blah blah blah…oh yeah!" Her eyes fell back on his. "The one thing I can't get over…the reason I've been acting like a lunatic…it's because I know once you start serving your sentence in prison, for however agonizingly long it may end up being, I'll have to work even harder than ever to prove to myself and everyone else that I'm still capable of making it on my own…even though part of me will die with every day we're apart." In that moment, her scripted speech evaporated, and she began to cry. "We might be crippled and gray by the time you're released! The locals will call me the 'Old Bag in One oh Seven' because the only way I'll be able to feel close to you will be by staying in this *shitty* motel room!"

When he reached out to pull her tight against him, a severe shiver ran down her spine despite the fact that his bare chest was giving off the heat of a furnace. She wasn't sure if it was because she was finally realizing their true connection, or if it was the start of hypothermia.

"I'm serving a year *tops* in the local jail," he stated calmly into her ear. "Luke is convinced it'll end up being no more than eight months with good behavior."

Her breath hitched as she arched away from him. "Come again?"

"The judge was sympathetic to my story…gave me two weeks to get my life in order. I figured the sentencing would be hard on you, so I'd planned to surprise you with something good along with the bad." Guilt darkened the light in his gaze. "I bought that little blue shack you're always drooling over, and I'm having it restored. The day you asked me to meet you and Cineste at your old man's place over the lunch hour, I had to meet with the contractor over some structural issues."

She couldn't believe what else he was saying. "Instead of telling me you were only spending a year in jail, you bought *the blue cottage*...the one on the beach?"

Eight months was manageable. He'd be out before Christmas. She wouldn't have to spend the next New Year alone after all.

"We both needed a change of scenery." He brushed a strand of hair away from her face, grinning in a way that made her dizzy. "You can settle in while I'm gone, get it set up the way you want. It'll be a good distraction to make the time we're apart go a little faster."

Drawing her lip between her teeth, she grinned. "Why does it feel like we've *both* lost our minds?"

"I already lost mine *months ago*...when a feisty little brunette with serious attitude came knocking on this same door. You've turned my entire world upside down, B. And I wouldn't want it any other way." He reached out to nudge her chin upward. "I had no clue you were this worried about my sentence. If I had, I wouldn't have held off telling you for this long. I'm sorry."

Her heart swelled with his well-meaning intentions. Even though he hadn't officially asked if she wanted to move in with him, nothing had ever felt so right. There weren't any pressures or fears that she wouldn't be a good roommate for him, unlike with Grayson. In the time she'd spent cohabitating with Brewer, they'd seamlessly accepted each other's bad habits and flaws. There wasn't a need for long, drawn-out conversation. Living together was a non-issue.

Holding back a smile, Bexley cocked her head. "Why *didn't* you tell me sooner?"

"I'd planned to tell you the night of the reunion…then you got the call about your old man. I worried you'd be even more upset once you knew I'd be gone soon. But I'm not going anywhere until I make damn sure the woman I love is settled in and taken care of."

Another shiver rippled down Bexley's core, shaking her entire body.

They'd both admitted they were in love.

"Come inside and let me warm you up," Brewer teased with a grin so sexy that Bexley felt it everywhere.

He gathered her in his brawny arms and carried her over the threshold, sliding his warm mouth over her frozen lips. She'd finally done it—

she'd exposed her darkest insecurities. And he still loved her.

---

BY THE TIME THEY CONGREGATED AROUND THE PLOT at the veterans' cemetery, the storm had passed and the skies were a lovely shade of blue. The greenery arranged around the simple urn on a pedestal glistened with rain drops that had yet to evaporate, and the birds chirped a happy song.

Bexley had been physically ill when she first learned Cineste arranged to have the captain buried beside their mother. Then she realized it gave her sister peace, and decided it wasn't worth another argument. Besides, their mother was blissfully unaware of their father's transgressions.

Bexley and Cineste stood near the non-denominational minister with their men at their sides. Aside from Kiersten, Luke, J.J., and a group of sailors in the ceremonial guard standing at attention nearby, there was no one else. No one who came solely to grieve for the captain rather than to comfort his daughters. It was both sad and fitting that so few mourned his death as so very few had respected him while living. Bexley found it ironic that someone may have despised him enough to have ended his life.

With every sniffle Cineste made, Bexley's annoyance simmered. She had neither informed her sister of their father's engagement, nor had she made any attempt to contact this "Kortney" after learning of the woman's existence. Bexley was harboring so much anger that it didn't leave room for sorrow, even when she recalled memories of being a little girl who loved her daddy.

As the sailors concluded the honors part of the service and the minister consoled Cineste, Bexley's friends circled around her. Each of them looked equally uncertain what to say. Under the circumstances, she couldn't blame them.

Considering Kiersten's complexion was a ghostly white in comparison to her black pants suit, Bexley figured she was dying to say something kind without irritating Bexley further. So Bexley stepped in to hug her. "Thank you for being my rock," she whispered. "I'm sorry I have been a shit friend—I haven't even congratulated you on your engagement."

Laughing softly, Kiersten's arms locked around Bexley. "I get it. You've been a little busy, my friend."

"I promise I'll make it up to you. I could throw you a party involving those tacky suckers you can sell, and a team of strippers disguised as lawyers."

"*That* won't be necessary!" Kiersten cackled.

Once Kiersten released her, Luke bent to kiss Bexley's cheek and offer his condolences.

Taking a hold of Luke's arm, Kiersten threw Bexley a warm smile. "We're going straight to the restaurant. Let us know if you need us to stop for anything."

"Unless we drink their bar dry, they should have everything we need," Bexley said with a wink. Kiersten kissed Bexley's cheek before they headed out.

J.J. dragged his portable oxygen tank closer to Bexley, then threw an arm around her shoulder. "I know you and your daddy had issues, darlin'," he wheezed, "but all things aside, it was a proper service for a man who served his country."

"I have nothing to say to that," Bexley confessed. "I feel like we just buried a stranger."

"Based on what you told me over the phone this mornin', that's understandable." J.J. paused to suck oxygen from the mask. "Lean heavy on this new fiancée. Surprise her with the news of your father's passing if she hasn't heard already, and find a way to monitor her reaction after you leave."

"That's an excellent idea."

Just then, Bexley spotted a young blonde woman in a white floral dress leaning against a large sycamore tree in the distance. It took all of five seconds for her memory to kick in, and realize the woman was her half-sister.

Bexley stiffened. Although she was relieved to know Cineste must've gotten ahold of Sadie, she also wasn't in the mood for a reunion. She never would've imagined the woman would have the courage to attend the service.

Sensing Bexley was distracted, Brewer cleared his throat and shook J.J.'s hand. "Thank you for coming. I know it's not easy for you to get around these days. Can I walk you to your car?"

J.J.'s shoulders lifted. "Just so long as you don't grab onto me like I'm an old woman."

"Go ahead, I'll catch up with you," Brewer told him. Then he wrapped his arm around Bexley's waist. "Maybe you should give her a chance," he whispered. "For all we know, you and Cineste are the only family she has left."

Turning to face him, Bexley grimaced. She'd been prepared to chastise him for guilting her into a confrontation with the woman, but he was so incredibly handsome in the same navy suit he'd worn on New Year's Eve that she easily caved. "Thank you for being here, Hawk. If it weren't for you, there's a fair chance I'd be covered in my own drool from psychotropic meds, and surrounded by padded walls."

His grin grew. "I planned on being here today no matter what your stubborn ass said or did to sabotage things." Chuckling, he set a hand beneath her ponytail to cradle her head, and kissed her forehead. "I'll make sure J.J. gets on his way while you talk to Sadie."

Bexley stepped away, awkwardly avoiding holes in the grass. She'd never been comfortable in heels, but Kiersten said they were essential with the elegant black dress they'd picked out together earlier that afternoon. The elbow-length sleeved midi fit and flair style was both comfortable and practical for a grieving daughter, but Bexley was itching to take it off and leave the memories of the day behind.

Once Sadie caught on to Bexley's intentions, her eyes widened and she spun around.

"Sadie, wait!" Bexley shouted. "You have every right to be here!"

Sadie paused, glancing over her shoulder. Without the garish makeup she'd worn the first time they'd met, she looked considerably younger and prettier. But as hard as Bexley tried, she didn't see any features that could be attributed to the captain. Sadie's face was narrow and petite, and her brown eyes were almost too big for their sockets.

"What do you *want*?" Sadie snapped.

"I'm not really sure," Bexley admitted, clasping her hands in front of her. "I guess I just felt like we should talk since we're sisters and everything."

Sadie shook her head. "That's funny, because you made it clear you want nothing to do with me when you ran after he introduced us."

"I was shocked to learn my father had been unfaithful to my mom. Did you really expect I'd pat him on the back and greet you with open arms?"

"Sadie," Cineste cooed, all at once standing beside Bexley. "I'm so glad you made it."

"I wasn't so sure I would." All at once, Sadie became sugary sweet with a toothy smile. "I flew standby. Luckily there were a few passengers that didn't show."

Detecting a slight Midwest accent, Bexley tilted her head. "Where did you fly in from?"

"Minneapolis," Sadie answered. "I live a couple hours from there."

*Minnesota*, Bexley thought. *The same place the*

*captain had been transferring sizable deposits.* Bexley set her hands on her hips, and gave the woman a threatening look. "If you came all this way expecting to inherit something, you're wasting your time. The captain filed bankruptcy before he died."

*"Bexley!"* Cineste scolded among a sharp gasp.

Bexley held Sadie's blank stare. "I mean you *were* getting money from him, right?"

"I don't know what you're talking about," Sadie snarled, suddenly taking on a defensive pose.

"Whoa!" Cineste tugged on Bexley's arm. "Why would you think he was giving her money, and what's this about *bankruptcy*?"

"I'll tell you everything later," Bexley promised, shrugging her off. Her gaze never unlocked with Sadie's. "We deserve to know why he was giving you a significant amount of money. Were you blackmailing him?"

"What's going on over here?" Alex asked in a protective voice, sliding in behind Cineste.

Bexley sensed Brewer stepping in behind her before she felt his comforting touch on the back of her waist. "Everything okay?"

With a sniffle, Cineste folded her arms over her waist. "Bex was just accusing our sister that we hardly know of bribing our father!"

"He was sending thousands of dollars to someone in Minnesota," Bexley informed her. "Kind of ironic that she lives there, don't you think?" She turned back to Sadie. "Are you really our sister? Do you have a blood test to prove it?"

"Maybe we should take this conversation somewhere else," Alex decided, motioning to a nearby group of mourners who had turned their way.

"Once I'm appointed executor of the captain's estate, I'll have the authority to call the bank to confirm it's your account," Bexley warned Sadie. "So may as well come clean about it now if you don't want any more hard feelings between us, *sis*."

"He was helping me pay off an important debt!" Sadie blurted. Her face turned scarlet red as she clutched her fists. "What does it matter, anyway? He was my dad too!"

It mattered to Bexley because someone else with a questionable motive had made her list of suspects.

# CHAPTER ELEVEN

Although Brewer implored her to take Friday morning off to tour *their* new home (a term she'd quickly adjusted to that secretly made her ridiculously giddy), Bexley swung by the office to confer with Red on a few things before heading downtown. Despite being painfully aware her remaining time with Brewer was stretching thin, she couldn't miss the opportunity to catch Elizabeth and Faye's thief red-handed.

Luxury cars peppered the parking lot facing a domed building that expanded across an entire city block on its own. The spa's lobby stretched three stories high, complete with a ceiling painted to resemble the Sistine Chapel. Bexley could practically *smell* the money that exchanged hands among the ornate light fixtures and diamond inlaid marble floors.

Bexley plopped down between two women who looked vaguely familiar despite the oversized sunglasses covering half their faces. She slipped her own smaller sunglasses from her handbag, and obscured her face behind a fashion magazine.

Nearly half an hour passed before she finally caught the big break she'd been hoping for. A 1990s version of Brad Pitt strolled through the waiting room, winking and nodding at every woman who caught his eye like he was actually the famous actor. Although he dressed the part of someone wealthy in crisp khaki pants, a cool white button-down, and trendy leather loafers, his honeyed blond hair was askew, and dark circles loomed beneath his engaging blue eyes. Young Brad was stressed.

Bexley tracked his progress to the receptionist's desk, then back to a seat across the wide room. He flirted with the woman beside him until she got up and moved across the room. With every minute that passed, more and more patients checked in until she could no longer monitor Young Brad. Luckily, she was able to see him rise to meet a thin blonde in a black lab coat, then disappear behind a set of doors. She quickly crossed the room to follow them, and wasn't stopped until seconds after she saw Young Brad ushered into one of the rooms.

"Can I help you?" the thin blonde in the lab coat asked.

Bexley surprised herself by answering in a Beverly Hills accent. "I've been waiting, like, *forever* in a room down the hall. Could you maybe direct me to the lady's room?"

The woman offered a stiff smile. "Of course. Down the hallway and to your left."

With a quick "thank you," Bexley followed the woman's directions. The restroom was conveniently located two doors down from Young Brad, and directly across from an askew door of a linen closet. Bexley snuck across and snagged one of the spa's black lab coats, then stowed her handbag beneath a large stack of towels.

Outside Young Brad's door, Bexley removed a manila file from a plastic sleeve and found the name: *Dexter O'Riley*. She tucked the file under her arm and stepped inside, discreetly locking the door behind her. Dexter was reclined in a patient's chair, fingers clasped over his stomach, completely unsuspecting of what was about to go down.

"Well hello, gorgeous," he greeted her, smiling.

"You must be new here. I'd remember that beautiful face in my dreams."

"Save it, Bra—Dexter," she quickly corrected herself. "Dammit, you even *look* like a Brad," she muttered under her breath.

"What'd you say?" he asked, tilting his head. "I swear I've seen you somewhere else."

*On a dating site, perhaps?* Bexley mused.

"I'm new alright." She picked up a corded tool that resembled a tooth grinder from a dentist's office, and flipped the power switch. Holding the vibrating instrument close to his groin, she shrugged. "What do you say we see what this sucker does?"

His Adam's Apple bobbed as he slid further back in the chair. "*What?*"

"Hand me your wallet," she demanded through gritted teeth.

"Wait. You're *robbing* me?"

"Although that would be the *actual* definition of irony, no. I just want to see your driver's license." Moving the spa's tool to her left hand, she slipped her stun gun from the smock's pocket with her right and held it up between them. "Don't make me use this."

"Shit—okay!" his trembling hand slipped into

his front pocket, and produced a thin leather wallet. "Here!"

Bexley set the tool down to take the wallet. She plucked the California license from the plastic window, and let the wallet drop to her feet. "Here's what's going to happen, *Dexter O'Riley*. Now that I know your real name and you don't have the luxury of anonymity, you're going to tell me what you did with Elizabeth Ricci's possessions."

Sliding farther up the back of the chair, he openly winced. "Who?"

"It's not in your best interests to play dumb, *Dex*, especially when you suck at acting." She slid the license into her pocket and retrieved the vibrating tool again, holding it within an inch of his face. "I'll bet this thing could put a big, ugly chip in the tip of your nose that even the best plastic surgeon couldn't repair. I should add my left hand isn't very coordinated, so who knows where it'll end up." Her finger slid the stun gun button, activating it in the air between them. "*This guy*, however, could inflict some serious damage to your overly active sex life. In fact, I'd be doing a lot of women a favor by putting you out of commission."

"Okay, *okay*!" Dexter yelped, his eyes expanding

with the current. "I'll tell you whatever you want to know! Just put that thing away!"

"Where are the things you stole from Elizabeth? Did you sell them?"

"Who would buy a weird looking key and a thumb drive?"

Bexley clicked her tongue. "What about the necklace, the handbag, the greenhouse?"

"The *what*? How could I steal an entire—"

"You're testing my patience, Dexter!" Bexley pressed the button on her stun gun again, moving it closer to his lap.

Dexter yelped in a feminine sound. "I swear, I don't know what you're talking about! I was only told to steal those two things!"

*Why would Elizabeth lie about what was stolen?* Bexley wondered. *Was she running an insurance scam?* "Who told you to steal them?"

"Did Elizabeth send you? Maybe you should ask *her* the whole story!"

"Your future kids are counting on you to be cooperative, Dexter!" She activated the stun gun within an inch of his groin. A dark patch of moisture spread over the crotch of his khakis.

His face crumpled, and he began to cry. "Alright! Jesus, lady, you're crazy!" He wiped at his face, sniffling. "About a month ago, I'd made plans to meet up with a woman through an anonymous dating site for rich assholes. When I got to the motel, I was jumped by two big dudes. They said they were onto my game, and knew about all the women I'd robbed. They threatened to take proof to the police unless I helped them."

"Did you see their faces?"

He shook his head. "They surprised me from behind and blindfolded me."

"Walk me through everything they said."

"One dude told me Elizabeth Ricci had stolen a thumb drive and key from him. He said I was going to run my usual scam to get into her apartment and steal them back. They told me I had two weeks to get it back to them or I could kiss my freedom goodbye."

Could it be true? Had Elizabeth hired Bexley only to get her hands on something that she had stolen in the first place?

Remembering Faye's story, she grimaced. "Your 'usual scam' is despicable, but we'll get to that later. How did you know where to find Elizabeth?"

"They left me with a manila envelope full of information...her picture, address, username on a hookup website."

"Do you still have the envelope?"

"I burned it after I returned the thumb drive and key."

"Where did you take them?"

"Back to the same motel."

"Which one?"

"This place called Big Dick's Inn. It's on—"

"I'm…familiar with it," Bexley huffed, rolling her eyes. As far as she was concerned, Brewer couldn't move out of that crime-infested rat's nest soon enough. "Did you hand them off to someone?"

"I was told to check in under the name 'Eddie Tolzman,' and lock them in the room's safe."

"Does that name mean anything to you?"

"Never heard it before."

Bexley scratched her head. "When was this?"

"Last Saturday. I haven't been able to sleep ever since because I keep expecting them to return."

"Now you know how your victims must feel," she snarled. The information wasn't the big revelation she'd been hoping for, but it sounded like Elizabeth hadn't disclosed everything when she'd hired Bexley. "Regarding the other women you conned… what have you done with the other items you stole?"

Dexter's eyes shifted to the doorway like he was hoping someone would come to his rescue.

"Come on, Dex. Now's not the time to get timid if you want the ability to walk away." Bexley sparked her stun gun one last time.

*"I sold it! The money is gone!"* he shouted. *"I spent it all on talent agents, and headshots!"*

The locked door handle jiggled. "Is everything okay in there?" a woman called out.

"Just sanding down a nasty mole!" Bexley hollered back. She wiggled the stun gun near his groin as a reminder of the power she held over him. "Nothing to worry about!" Leaning down to Dexter's eye level, she shot him a warning glare. *"Promise me* you're done conning women on dating sites so I don't have to come after your family jewels again!"

More tears tumbled from Dexter's eyes. "I promise! *I promise!"*

Discarding the tool, Bexley lifted the large pendant on a chain around her neck that she'd borrowed from Red. "Smile for the camera, Dexter O'Riley. This could be your big shot at becoming famous."

His wet eyes rounded. "You're joking."

"With a face this serious?" She held the stun

gun in front of his face in warning. "Your career as a criminal is over, Dexter."

EN ROUTE TO ELIZABETH RICCI'S CONDO, BEXLEY swallowed her misgivings and swung by the Papaya Springs police station. The curious stares of Grayson's coworkers seared against her skin. She hadn't been there since their breakup, and was convinced he'd turn her away. When he stomped out to meet her in the lobby, nostrils flaring as he waited for her to explain herself, she felt sick to her stomach. He wasn't the same man she'd treasured for so many months.

"Can we talk in your office?" she pleaded. "I have something important to show you."

He let out a heavy sigh, then motioned for her to follow. Having forgotten about his promotion, she nearly tripped when he continued past his office toward the lieutenant's. She entered the larger room behind him, awkwardly standing beside his desk. The walls had a fresh coat of white paint, but there wasn't anything to personalize it beyond a set of plaques bearing Grayson's name. Bexley suddenly felt sad he didn't deem any memories worth framing.

He closed the door and turned to her, crossing his arms over his chest. "What do you want from me this time, Bex?"

"I'm here as a professional courtesy. I won't take up much of your time." She removed the necklace Red had given her, and slid the tiny memory card from its compartment. "Is a confession on video enough to bring someone in for questioning related to a string of thefts?"

"Depends. Was this confession coerced? Was the video taken without their knowledge?"

"Maybe a little of both? But I was involved in the conversation." Bexley handed the small card to him. "Can you please at least take a look, and see if there's anything you can do? This man has been stealing from women he meets through dating sites."

Grayson stared at the card in the palm of his hand. "I owe you an apology for how things went down at the reunion," he blurted. His eyes slowly dragged back up to meet hers. "I'd obviously been drinking too much that night."

Nodding, Bexley ran her bottom lip through her teeth. "It's not like you to get that way."

His expression softened. "Kiersten told me about the captain. How are you handling it?"

"I wouldn't say 'great'. He was living a secret life, and I have a reason to believe that his death wasn't an accident."

Rubbing a hand over his eyes, Grayson huffed. "You never were good with emotions. Are you sure this isn't just your way of dealing with his death—by looking for something that may not be there? Wouldn't it be better to let him rest in peace?"

A sense of closure took Bexley by surprise. Grayson may have *loved* her wholeheartedly, but he'd never truly *believed in* her. Not like Brewer. "Take care of yourself, Gray."

———

Upon entering Elizabeth Ricci's condo, Bexley barely took notice of the 20-foot ceilings, whitewashed living spaces, modern light fixtures, sparkling tile floors, and walls of glass overlooking the ocean. She was over the extravagant lives of the elite in Papaya Springs, and couldn't wait to move into their cozy little shack by the ocean.

After letting Bexley in, Elizabeth strode to the kitchen. She wore a long white kimono over ripped jean shorts and a rose colored satin tank top, and her golden hair was piled in a messy bun on top of her head. "Can I get you something to drink? I was just going to open a bottle of wine."

"I'm good, thanks," Bexley answered, fighting an eye roll. Wine before noon on a weekday was a foreign concept to her.

Elizabeth plucked a dark bottle from a stainless steel wine cooler, and retrieved an electric opener. "I'm assuming you're here because you have good news."

Bexley leaned against the concrete island between them, arms crossed. "I caught up with your friend 'Brad', real name Dexter O'Riley. He's a real piece of work."

Elizabeth set the opener down with excitement filling her eyes. "Did you recover my things?"

"That's the funny thing, Elizabeth." Bexley strode across the open floor plan to perch on the edge of a pristine white couch. "He claims he only took the key and a thumb drive."

"And you believed him?"

Bexley folded her arms and lifted one brow. "Considering the circumstances surrounding his confession? Yeah, I do. He was told the key unlocked something of great importance."

"Does it matter what it unlocks?"

"Possibly, considering he was also told *you* had stolen the key *from someone else*."

With her mouth in a tight line, Elizabeth grabbed two large wine glasses from a cabinet, and began to poor the red liquid in each.

"I'm really not much of a day drinker," Bexley grumbled. "Especially when I'm *trying* to do *my job* even though my client appears to be withholding valuable information."

"As *your client*, I insist." Elizabeth handed her one of the half full glasses, and scowled. "Besides, you're going to be here for awhile if you want the whole story."

# PART II

# CHAPTER TWELVE

## HOLLYWOOD HILLS, CALIFORNIA

AUGUST 15TH

Elizabeth Ricci sensed she was in serious trouble long before she crept into her parents' sprawling 5 acre estate. She'd been out all night with a man her father had never met.

Even if the two *had* met, her infamous crime lord father would never deem Barnett Freeberg good enough for his 24-year-old daughter. In Mattia Ricci's eyes, *no one* could ever fit that bill. And once Barnett discovered Elizabeth was the "princess" of a mob boss, he wouldn't want anything to do with her ever again. It had happened with every single guy she'd dated since she was fifteen. The threats that came with dating a murderous man's daughter were too much for any of her suitors to handle. So in the five months they'd been together, she'd resolved to never let the two men meet.

Barnett was everything Elizabeth ever wanted in a boyfriend…smart, successful, handsome, and heir to a fortune equal—if not greater—to her own. When the day came that she finally found a husband and left home, she wasn't going to settle for anything less than the posh lifestyle she'd known. Helicopters to avoid L.A. traffic, trips around the world in private jets, and luxury cars worth no less than six digits were her norm.

As Barnett's father ran one of the most successful computer corporations in the Bay Area, he was accustomed to the same way of life. His family owned vacation homes in Hawaii, Lake Tahoe, Venice, and New York. Barnett, a recent Harvard graduate, worked under his dad. He leased a $5M loft in downtown L.A. and drove an Aston Martin. In less than a decade, he was expected to become the CEO of his dad's corporation, and could become one of the youngest billionaires in the world.

By all accounts, he was perfect.

Elizabeth was in love.

"Where have you been, young lady?" her

father's voice boomed from behind her as she was opening the door to her bedroom suite.

"The house in Papaya Springs. A few friends stopped over for drinks, and I fell asleep."

He grunted. "Security would've notified me if you'd been there. Try again."

Her entire body tensed. Lying to Mattia Ricci usually produced unsavory consequences. "I was clubbing with friends."

"Until five in the morning?"

Snorting, she turned to face him. "Yes, Daddy. It's called being an adult, and knowing how to have a good time."

For as far back as she could remember, she'd adored her father. In a black robe and bare feet, he looked uncharacteristically vulnerable, and nothing like the don of a criminal organization. He'd begun to noticeably shrink since turning 60. In addition, deep wrinkles surrounded his eyes, and his dark hair had receded completely off the top of his head. At least he had the same pudgy cheeks and round belly she'd seen jiggle with laughter countless times throughout her childhood. His big brown eyes usually shone with love for his little girl, but not that night.

There had been a major shift between them

ever since she'd turned twenty, and spent more time out with friends and suitors than she spent at home. Her father had tightened her weekly allowance, hoping it would keep her on a shorter leash, and made her check in wherever she went. Considering most of her friends had important jobs and owned their own homes, she was embarrassed. And she hated that her father always assumed she was up to no good.

"Don't get smart with me," he warned, wagging his finger. "Do I need to ask Vinnie to start keeping a tail on you?"

"You wouldn't dare." Vinnie Romano was her father's best friend of 50 years, and his right-hand man. Elizabeth regarded him as a pesky uncle who was always poking his nose in her business even more than her own father. "I'm not some little girl who needs babysitting!"

"Then stop acting like it!" her father roared, face tight with anger. "I have too many enemies in this town! Do I have to remind you how many threats there have been on your life? I can't afford to lose you while you're off gallivanting around all hours of the night!"

"Can't *afford* to lose me?" she repeated. "I'm not one of your investments!"

With a violent shake of his head, her father grunted. "From now on, you will be home by midnight! And if you break curfew, I'm sending Vinnie *everywhere* as your bodyguard!"

"I'd like to see you try!" she roared back at him before slamming her bedroom door.

He banged on the door, demanding she let him in, but she engaged the lock and leaned against it. She was done letting him treat her like a child.

# CHAPTER THIRTEEN
## PAPAYA SPRINGS, CALIFORNIA

**SEPTEMBER 8TH**

Following the night she finally stood up to her father, Elizabeth spent several weeks at their family's $10M beach house in Papaya Springs. Her parents only came to the property during summer months, so she didn't have to worry about them ruining her fun. But there was always a dark sedan parked across the street, watching her every move.

She invited Barnett to spend the night as often as his work schedule would allow. They'd make love on the deck overlooking the ocean, and drink wine late into the night while planning their future together. One chilly night as they were wrapped around each other on the 20' outdoor couch with

Italian cushions as soft as clouds, moon dancing over the calm ocean while Michael Bublé serenaded them from speakers hidden around the deck, Barnett blindsided her with a request.

"I want to meet your parents," he said in a voice as smooth as maple syrup. "I want to shake your father's hand."

Meeting her father was the only subject that could've ruined the blissfully sweet night. "Trust me, you don't," she said with a dismissive laugh, bending to kiss the tip of his pointed nose. "They're literally *the worst*." She actually wasn't too far off base. While her father made his fortune by swindling and ordering hits on his enemies, her mother blew wads of his money with her stuck up friends like it was toilet paper.

Barnett stared at her with captivating eyes the same color as the ocean. Six feet tall, slightly muscular, full lips, luscious chocolate brown hair, he was the kind of traditionally handsome that stopped women in their tracks. When Elizabeth had first spotted him at the yacht club landing a dinghy, shirtless and deeply tanned, she'd finally understood the definition of "love at first sight." He'd been courting another woman at the time, but that didn't stop Elizabeth from getting what she wanted.

"Trust me, Lizzy, I want to meet them." His expression became gravely serious as he cradled her face in his hands. "I need to ask for their permission to marry you."

Elizabeth gasped. "Are you being serious right now?"

With a wide smile, he took her hands in his. "No one has ever made me this happy. I want to spend every day until I die with you by my side, Elizabeth Roserio."

Letting out a squeal, she tackled him down to his back and sealed her lips over his. The fact that he didn't know her real name, or that she was the only offspring of Papaya Spring's most powerful kingpin, weighed heavily on her mind. Although the white lie seemed necessary in the beginning, she never dreamed it'd continue on for so long. Since Barnett's family certainly would've performed a background check on any woman who came sniffing around, she'd hired the best hacker in the business to create a false history under that name.

Breathless, Barnett removed his mouth from hers. "So when can I meet them?"

"They're overseas for at least a few months." Her eyes skipped over to the ocean. "I'm not exactly sure when they're coming back."

"We can fly to wherever they're staying. We could even surprise them." He chuckled and tucked a lock of her hair behind her ear. "Sweetheart, I can afford to take you anywhere you want. Maybe even the moon."

"I'm not so sure that's a good idea. My dad isn't big on surprises." She rose to her feet, collecting their empty glasses. "I'll open another bottle."

"I'll get it." Barnett came jogging after her, taking the glasses away. "Why do I feel like you're blowing this off? Are you embarrassed by me?"

"That's just ridiculous." She stood on her toes to give him a soft kiss. "If anything, I'm embarrassed by my parents." She looked away, unable to lie directly to his face. "They're…not what you'd imagine."

He released a throaty laugh. "Unless they're paupers and you've simply been squatting in this house, I highly doubt that. Babe, what could possibly be embarrassing about the people who raised the woman I love and adore? Are they ogres? *Democrats?*"

Elizabeth wanted to fall to her knees and cry. Their chance at happiness would be doomed the moment Barnett stepped foot on her parents' property in Hollywood Hills. He'd learn that she'd been lying to him since the day they met, and he'd discover her family's darkest secrets.

She clasped his forearms as an idea sparked in her belly. "Let's elope! We can leave right now and get married somewhere romantic like the top of the Eiffel Tower, or a vineyard in Italy!"

"No. *No way*. I'm giving you the kind of elegant, over-the-top wedding all women dream of as girls. My parents will insist we invite everyone who's anyone." He pulled her arms down and clasped their fingers together. "I want to look your father in the eye, and let him know I plan to take care of his little girl."

Dread rippled through Elizabeth's stomach. She had a sixth sense that their introduction would be disastrous, only she had no idea it would be on a life-changing level.

# CHAPTER FOURTEEN

## HOLLYWOOD HILLS, CALIFORNIA

SEPTEMBER 10TH

The last time Elizabeth brought a man home to meet her parents, he hadn't even made it through dinner. It had been a little less than a year since she'd witnessed A.J.'s cowardly side. Once her father set a gun on the table and warned he wouldn't let anyone get by with hurting his daughter, A.J. had excused himself from the table. A handful of seconds later, they'd heard his Ferrari's tires squealing on the pavement outside. Turns out her father ended up doing her a favor because she discovered A.J. was sleeping with other women the entire time they were together.

Barnett was different in every way imaginable.

He was faithful and as kind as any man had ever been to Elizabeth. The only flaws he'd shown in the nearly six months they'd been together were small enough to be overlooked. Elizabeth was certain he was meant to be the father of her children, which made it almost impossible to willingly step inside her parents' home.

They entered the house, hand-in-hand. Since they'd pulled up to the estate, Barnett had been oddly quiet. Deciding her nervous energy was rubbing off on him, Elizabeth nudged him and smiled. "They're going to love you to pieces," she assured him, even though it was a delusional wish.

He took a deep breath, and parted his lips to say something the same time Elizabeth's parents came into the parlor to greet them.

The moment they came face-to-face, Barnett and her father reacted simultaneously. It was as if a sudden storm with deafening thunder and lethal lightening had caught them all by surprise.

Elizabeth felt as if the scene unfolded in slow motion. Her father's face flushed. He bolted forward. "What the hell are *you* doing here?" he demanded. "How *dare* you set foot inside my home!" He reached beneath his blazer.

With a sharp gasp, Elizabeth's mother grasped

her husband's wrist, stopping him from drawing his weapon. "Not here, Mattia! I just had the floors redone from the last time you lost your temper on one of our guests!"

Barnett's face had taken on the same dark red shade as her father's. For a heartbreaking moment, Elizabeth feared the love of her life would rush at her father. Then Barnett's expression evened out, and all color drained from his face. His ocean-blue eyes flicked between the father and daughter before his shoulders drooped.

"This *bastard* is your father?" he snarled at Elizabeth. "You told me your last name was Roserio!"

Elizabeth's stomach fell to her feet as tears rushed to her eyes. "What's happening? How do you know each other?"

"Step away from my daughter!" her father ordered, brandishing his gun.

"Daddy!" Elizabeth cried, flattening herself against Barnett. "Put that away!"

"Do you have any idea who you're defending, young lady?" her father roared. "Do you have any clue what this man's father did?"

Barnett shoved Elizabeth out of the way, and took one step closer to the mobster. "What *my father* did? You bastard! *You* stole everything from my uncle! It's your fault he drank himself to death!"

Elizabeth's father raised a clenched fist in the air. "He did that to himself! He was a madman! He threatened to kill my baby girl!"

Her head spun. *What was her father saying?* When Barnett turned to glance at Elizabeth over his shoulder, pausing to lick his lips, she could sense deep remorse.

"Is that why you're here?" her father continued. "Were you sent to seduce her before carrying out your father's orders?"

"What's he talking about?" Elizabeth whispered, gripping Barnett's arm. "Please, baby! Answer me!"

Barnett turned her way, his beautiful face a ghostly white, eyes placid.

The quiet click of the safety being released drew their attention back to her father. He gripped the gun in both hands, aiming it at Barnett's head. "You have ten seconds to leave this house before I put a bullet between your eyes!"

Shaking her head, Elizabeth backed against the wall and wrapped her arms around herself. They were both lying. They *had to* be. She couldn't accept that the family of the man she wanted to spend her life with was involved in an unforgivable history with her family.

"Stop!" Elizabeth pleaded, throwing her hands over her ears. "No more! I can't take this!"

The air whooshed from her lungs when Barnett turned and stormed toward the front door. She'd expected him to tell her that there had been a mistake, and he *hadn't* been sent to kill her. She'd wanted him to tell her not to worry, that they'd find a way to move on without their families. At the very least, she prayed he'd beg her to run away with him.

Barnett didn't profess his undying love, nor did he make a scene about being ejected. He didn't even bother glancing her way. It was over.

Elizabeth's legs gave out beneath her.

# CHAPTER FIFTEEN

L ater that night, Elizabeth forced Vinnie to tell her everything about the beef between the two families. According to her father's oldest friend, Barnett's uncle and her father had roomed together in college, and remained close after graduation. Several decades later, her father had given Barnett's family seed money to start their spyware corporation. Once Barnett's father and uncle discovered the mob was running business through the corporation, they'd requested to buy Elizabeth's father out. Vinnie claimed her father refused to accept anything less than ten million in addition to his original investment, and the three men began a five-year argument that escalated with death threats against Elizabeth.

She was tired of her father's shady business practices interfering with her life.

She was done with the Ricci name, and done living under the dark shadow of Mattia Ricci's legacy.

But first, she wanted revenge.

She locked herself inside her Hollywood Hills bedroom suite for days, refusing to interact with either of her parents. Whenever they were both gone, she'd rifle through every nook and cranny of the house, looking for the stacks of dirty money she was certain her father was hiding from the government.

In order to run away, she would need a fat stack of cash. The $10k in her bank account wouldn't last her more than a month.

By the time she remembered the secret room behind her father's office, she was beside herself with annoyance. How could she have forgotten the place she once thought she'd die in when she'd been little?

Her heartbeat raced as she recalled that fateful day…the sound of the steel door slamming shut behind her…the crippling darkness of the window-less room…the endless tears she shed once her empty stomach began to growl…the hysteria that filled her four-year-old head when she was convinced there was a monster in the room with her…

As Elizabeth would learn in later years, the room had been built in the mid 1800s during the gold rush. Its intentions were two-fold: (1) to protect the proprietor's stash of gold, and (2) to lock any burglars inside who were able to find a way in.

She never heard how her parents found her, but she'd never been so relieved to see them in her short time on earth. When she thought back to memories of that day, it dawned on her that she'd subconsciously avoided his office ever since.

A chill covered her skin as she entered the vast wing of the house. Because of her father's ongoing battle with obesity, he was always overheated and preferred to blast the cold air no matter the temperature outside. As Elizabeth stepped inside the office lined in dark walnut, she rubbed her hands together to ward off the cold. It was almost exactly as she remembered it—dark and dreary with century old furniture bearing ornate accents, thick with the rich scent of the hundreds of ancient books lining the dozens and dozens of tall shelves.

Memories from all those years ago came rushing back with clarity. After she'd been rescued, her father had secured the room with a strange little key. Then he'd looked over his shoulder to ensure that no one was watching, and placed it inside a little metal box. He hadn't noticed Elizabeth in the corner of the room, peering out from the blanket her mother had wrapped her in before speaking with the police officers in the hallway.

She approached the desk and opened the drawer, felt around the topside until her fingers came into contact with a small metal box.

*Bingo.*

With a pleased smile, she slid the little box open and removed its contents.

The antique brass key, lined with unusual notches and decorated with a complex pattern, was unexpectedly beautiful. It felt surprisingly light in the palm of Elizabeth's hand.

To an outsider, the secret door was unde-tectable. She had only found it when she was little because her father had left it open a crack. Drawing from the memories she had buried long ago, she raced across the room to one of the dark panels. In the same manner as her father had done all those years ago, she rotated a loose piece of trim to reveal a lock.

Her pulse quickened as she inserted the key.

It turned with a quiet *click*.

CHAPTER SIXTEEN

The secret room was half the size Elizabeth had remembered—to the point she felt the tendrils of claustrophobia squeezing her throat when she peered into the dark, musty space. Not willing to repeat the incident from her childhood, she shoved a heavy coffee table against the open door before heading inside.

The walls were lined in metal so thick that she understood why her mother told the police they hadn't heard her cries for help. For all intents and purposes, it was a fortress.

Less than a dozen corrugated cardboard boxes were stacked throughout the room. Elizabeth began flipping their lids open to dig through their contents. She found envelopes with her father's name written in a flourishing cursive and continued on, assuming they contained love letters her mother had written when they first dated decades ago. It seemed the boxes were filled with nothing more than keepsakes. There were tickets to concerts and playbills, boarding passes and hotel key cards.

Skeptical that her father was merely sentimental, and there wasn't a darker purpose to the collection, she continued digging. The last thing she came across was an empty black velvet box. With a heavy sigh, she admitted defeat. There didn't appear to be *anything* of value inside the room. Her father was too smart to have kept embezzled cash within reach. He would've invested in accounts overseas like every other criminal in the free world.

As she bent to return the black box to the stack of other useless memorabilia, something rattled inside. She pushed on the sides of the box, discovering a false bottom. Her fingers slid it open to reveal a thumb drive. *Must be something important,* Elizabeth decided.

The deep roll of a man's voice came from the hallway. In a moment of panic, she dropped the thumb drive into her pocket and hurried from the room, also pocketing the key after the room was secured. She then swiped a random book off a shelf and meandered into the hallway, almost colliding with Vinnie.

"Whoa! What ya doin' kiddo?" he asked, folding his arms over his wide chest. Unlike her father, Vinnie was thick with muscle, tall, and considerably attractive for a man in his sixties. His eyes reminded her of a basset hound's—sad and sweet at the same time.

She held the book up. "Finding something constructive to pass the time before I go to my grave an old spinster."

"You still tore up about your pops and that kid?"

"Of course! I love Barnett!" Anger swept through her limbs, curling her fists. "Why do you do it, Vinnie? Why do you continue to work for my father after all these years, knowing he'd do anything to protect his precious fortune—without caring who he hurt in the process?"

Vinnie scrubbed at his square jaw with his hand, thick black eyebrows drawn down. "Your pops and me go way back, kiddo. We're like blood brothers. Other than my sweet Gloria, who's my entire world, he's all I got left. You're my family. There ain't nothin' I wouldn't do to protect every one of ya from harm. There's no messin' with a bond that solid. We look out for each other at all costs…ya know? And that's why I understand where your pops is comin' from. If I were him, I would've gutted that little Freeberg prick for what he did to ya."

With a sad shake of her head, Elizabeth returned to her bedroom suite where she opened her laptop and inserted the thumb drive.

Reality slipped away from beneath her as a video began to play.

She could never unsee the images flashing across the screen.

Her father had made a sex tape.

With Vinnie's wife Gloria.

# PART III

# CHAPTER SEVENTEEN

## PAPAYA SPRINGS, CALIFORNIA

JANUARY 3RD

Gulping down her third serving of red wine, Elizabeth set the empty glass on the concrete island in front of Bexley. "I'm close with one of the younger maids, and I asked her to spy on my father after I left. Once I told him I'd taken the video and key, she said he panicked and tried having a duplicate made, but he wasn't able to find a locksmith experienced enough to work with the antique lock. She said a contractor came by the house next, and told him the steel walls were completely impenetrable. Then my parents got into a huge fight because apparently he'd told my mother that the room was filled in after I'd been locked inside. Once I realized how desperate he'd become to protect his dirty little secret, I spent months doing my best to bleed his bank account dry. There wasn't a limit to what he'd pay in order to prevent my mom and Vinnie from seeing the video and the contents of that room. Turns out none of it was from my mom—they were all keepsakes involving Gloria. They've been sleeping together for decades." Her eyes drifted away from Bexley's. "I figured he'd get his hands on the thumb drive and key sooner or later—only I guessed it would be later, and hadn't taken the time to make a copy of the video. At least I blew his money on the most ridiculous things you could imagine when I had the chance. I wanted to hit him where it hurt."

Bexley carefully considered her response. As much as she could empathize with Elizabeth's situation, as an outsider she was able to see the bigger picture. "How do you see this ending? Do you think your father put the key back where you found it, and kept those videos in the same hiding place? They're more than likely long gone by now."

"Then I'll threaten to tell Vinnie and my mother!" Elizabeth snapped, crossing her arms over her chest.

"Are you sure you want to go that route? It

sounds to me like Vinnie's loyalties to your father are rock solid. Do you think he'll believe your allegation if you don't have anything to prove it?"

Elizabeth's perfectly glossed lips quivered before she tightened them again. "Vinnie has always been good to me. I don't want to hurt him, but he deserves to know."

Bexley took a deep breath before setting her hand over the younger woman's. "I'm sorry about Barnett, Elizabeth. I imagine you felt betrayed by both him and your father. I could be wrong, but… the way things went down, I can't help wondering if there's still a chance to fix things between you and Barnett. Have you reached out to him since that night? I mean, you said he appeared genuinely surprised to learn who you were, and he never actually confirmed that he was sent after you like your father claimed. What if he was just too shocked that you had lied to him, and needed time to realize *why* you did it?"

A spark of hope lit Elizabeth's expression. "You think?"

"I think it's worth a shot. If you want, I can arrange something. I could even come along as a mediator of sorts."

With a stuttered breath, Elizabeth's shoulders

fell. "You wanna know what *I* think?" A little smirk spread across her glossy pink lips. "I'm actually starting to like you, Bexley Squires."

After jumping through several hoops with Barnett's office staff, Bexley finally arranged for the star-crossed lovers to meet the following Monday. Of course Barnett didn't know the exact details of the meeting, but he'd been more than interested to meet with the private investigator who claimed to have insider knowledge about his ties to Mattia Ricci.

Once Brewer had secured special permission from his parole agent to leave the state for a night, Bexley boarded a plane for Oregon early Saturday morning with him at her side. It'd been his idea to tag along, and she was secretly thrilled. She wanted to keep him close while he was still around.

"What's that?" Brewer asked, motioning to the dime-sized electronic device Bexley fidgeted with during the flight.

She turned to him and winked. "Super-secret spy stuff."

His eyes danced with mischief. "Does that mean

you're going to wear one of those tight leather catsuits female spies always wear in the movies?"

"Only in your dreams, buddy."

"Oh…you have no idea the kind of dreams I have about you, B. *Trust* me."

Nudging his ribcage with her elbow, she held it out for his inspection. "It's one of Red's inventions. I'm hoping to plant it on something of Kortney's so I can listen in on her *real* reaction to my ambush."

"Isn't that…illegal?"

"Only if I'm caught."

"Dang. I was hoping maybe we'd end up doing time together." He chuckled and nudged her back.

The joke stole her breath for a fraction of a second. While she was glad he still possessed enough humor to make light of his situation, she hated the constant reminder that he was going away. She eyed him thoughtfully, deciding the ease of their bond had become one massive breath of fresh air. Maybe he was merely trying to help her accept his fate.

"If there's anything I can do to help while we're here, just say the word," he offered. "I'm no PI, but I know a thing or two about being stealthy." Smirking, he wiggled his eyebrows. "I'd be more than happy to do a little secret spy shit with you, Squires."

"Hold that thought." Grinning, she leaned back in the airplane seat and closed her eyes. "It's my turn to picture *you* in a tight leather suit."

———

STEPPING INTO THE CASINO'S SPA WAS AKIN TO entering a tropical paradise. Between potted palm trees, bamboo trim, the scent of plumeria, and Hawaiian guitar music drifting through the air, Bexley was reminded she was past due for a vacation. She almost wished she was there for a real massage, and not as a rouse to corner the captain's newest catch.

Once again, she used the old "needing a bathroom" trick to gain access to the employee's locker room. Several times she was forced to hide when someone entered. She rifled through six different lockers before finding a purse with Kortney Lockhart's driver's license. She took a picture of the license before positioning the listening device inside the small, brown leather crossbody bag, and hoped Kortney wasn't the type to leave her purse in her car.

She hadn't returned to the waiting room for long before a young, lithe blonde who appeared to have the flexible range of a Cirque du Soleil performer appeared to announce the bogus name Bexley had used to make the appointment. Bexley studied the young woman, telling herself she hadn't been too far off base when she'd met their half-sister, and assumed *she'd* been her father's newest lover. Ever since Bexley's mother passed away, the captain had been going for younger and younger women.

Despite having an impressive figure and youthful appearance, Bexley sensed the woman had already lived a hard life. She wasn't as polished as the receptionist or the other masseuses that had passed through the lobby. There was a hardness to her bright green eyes, and her skin was rough like that of a heavy smoker. Bexley didn't want to jump to rash conclusions, but she sensed Kortney could also be a drug user by the dark spots and blemishes on her face. Empty piercings marked one eyebrow, her nose, and running up both earlobes. Her blond hair looked tired the way it hung limp from her petite head, its highlights in dire need of refreshing.

Banking on the fact that the captain wouldn't have disclosed to his newest conquest that he had daughters older than her, Bexley popped to her feet. "That's me."

"Great! I'm Kortney," she answered in a low, scratchy voice. "Follow me."

As they started down a quiet hallway, Bexley spotted several tattoos beneath the spa's white tunic dangling off Kortney's bony shoulders. She was nothing like the captain's past two wives, who had been both flawless and attractive by modern standards.

Bexley stepped into the room past her, immediately overwhelmed by the strong sent of incense and gentle sounds of a piano playing among chirping birds. It was dark except for a small lamp glowing from a narrow table with a vase of bright flowers and a small water fountain.

"Go ahead and take your clothes off, then lay face down on the table," Kortney instructed, letting the door close behind her. "There's a sheet on the counter you can cover yourself with, if it'd make you more comfortable. I'll give you a few minutes to settle in."

Bexley choked down a laugh. In the event she was forced to chase after Kortney, she preferred *not* to do it naked. "Actually, Kortney, I'm here to talk to you about Dominic Ferguson."

Stone-faced, the young woman batted her short, mascara-clumped eyelashes. "What *about* him? Who are you?"

"I'm his daughter."

"Is that a fact?" Arms tightly coiled around her concave stomach, Kortney flexed her jaw. "Why are you here? What do you want?"

"Is it true about you and the captain?" Bexley prodded. "Are you engaged?"

"Why don't you ask your dad?"

Apparently she *didn't* know the captain had died. Remembering J.J.'s advice, Bexley decided to string the woman along before resorting to the element of surprise. "I'm asking you."

Kortney's eyes narrowed. "Look, lady. If you're here to tell me you don't approve of us getting married, you can march right back out the door. He's a grown man. Whatever he does is *his* business and no one else's. Ain't no one gonna tell us what we can and can't do."

"That's not what this is, I swear." With her hands held up, Bexley sat on the edge of the table. She needed to appear less combative before Kortney decided to bolt. "If you're going to be in his life, I wanted to take the time to get to know you better."

"You serious?"

"As a heart attack!" Smiling brightly, Bexley leaned forward with her chin on one hand and tried to muster the kind of bright attitude she imagined it took to engage in "girl talk." "I want to know everything! How'd the two of you meet?"

With a snorting laugh, Kortney motioned to where Bexley sat. "You're lookin' at it."

"He came to the casino often?"

"Every weekend. I think he comes here to get away. When I first met him, he seemed like a really lonely guy."

*Except that he was married,* Bexley wanted to say. "Ah, in that case, I'm so glad you found each other! How many times did you give him a massage before he asked you out?"

Kortney's eyes shifted to the corner of the room. "I dunno…a couple."

Bexley smelled a lie. Had Kortney been giving the captain more than an innocent massage from day one? Bexley shuddered with the thought. "How did he ask you to marry him? Was he super romantic?"

"Yeah." Kortney's hand movements became flighty, tugging at her tunic and twisting in her hair. "I mean…I guess."

"He must *really* like the slot machines to come here that often."

"Not so much." Kortney lifted one shoulder. "He's more of a sports betting kind of guy."

"He bet on professional teams?"

"Yeah…here in the casino."

"Is that how he lost all his money?"

Kortney shuffled backwards, her expression pinched with confusion. "I don't—"

"Come on, Kortney." Bexley stood, crowding the young woman until she was trapped in the corner. "You're engaged to marry the man. Are you seriously going to tell me you didn't know he'd filed for bankruptcy?"

"All I know is he's in deep with his bookie!" she sputtered, sucking her cheeks in. "He owes the guy hundreds of thousands of dollars!"

"Did you agree to marry him before or *after* you learned he was in debt?"

"Before!" Her darting gaze pinned Bexley in place as her voice hardened. "But it doesn't matter! I'm marrying him because we're in love! He tells me I'm his rock!"

Bexley's patience was thinning. "If that's true, when did you last see him?"

"I don't know! A week? He was supposed to

come and see me last Saturday, but I haven't heard from him since!"

"Aren't you worried?" Bexley drew in a slow, steady breath. "If it's been a week, why are you at work instead of out actively looking for him? Have you called the cops? Do you even know where he lives?"

Kortney's face reddened. "Why are you asking me all these questions? What's going on?"

"Your *fiancé* is dead, Kortney. He was killed in a car crash last weekend, and I'm pretty sure it wasn't an accident."

For a drawn-out moment, Kortney's eyes widened and her lips trembled. "Oh no," she whispered. "He can't be. Please tell me it isn't true."

"We buried him on Thursday. You weren't notified because, well, the captain never mentioned you." Bexley stared at the girl a beat longer, waiting for her eyes to well with tears, or her to crumple to the floor with grief. But nothing happened beyond the jittery movement of her eyes, and her hand covering her mouth.

CHAPTER EIGHTEEN

While Brewer kept an eye on Kortney's beater car in the parking lot, Bexley paid a visit to Frank Jones, the casino's bookie. Although the 50-something-year-old man with thinning hair and a nervous tick that pulled at his bird-like features didn't have much to say about Bexley's father, he was soon ranting about how eager he was to collect on the captain's debt.

She cut him off by asking, "Did you know he'd filed for bankruptcy?"

"What does that have to do with anything? Don't mean his debts with me were forgiven."

"As you said *several* times, two hundred thousand is a steep debt. I'll bet you were angry when you learned you weren't going to get your money back. Maybe even angry enough to want him dead."

Frank wiped at his forehead. "Lady, that there's just crazy talk. How would he pay me back if he was dead?"

"Where were you early last Saturday morning?"

"Are you kidding?" Frank's nostrils flared. "I'm married to this place. I was *right here*, hosting a going away party for one of my co-workers. We started the party Friday after work…didn't leave until six a.m."

Bexley's stomach churned as she tapped her boot over the casino's thin carpet. She was getting close to the truth—she could feel it.

It'd be easy enough to corroborate Frank's alibi with casino security footage, and she imagined there had been a large handful of witnesses. But it didn't mean he hadn't hired someone to take her father out. If Kortney proved to be a dead end, she'd dig more into Frank's background.

"Do you know anyone else in the casino who may've been on the outs with Captain Ferguson?"

Frank scratched his chin. "Aside from owing me money, he was a decent guy. Doubt there's anyone who had a bone to pick with 'em." Eyes shifting around the room, he tugged at the neck of his dress shirt. "What's this about, anyway? Do I need me a lawyer?"

Her phone buzzed in her handbag. She fished it out to discover Brewer was calling.

"Thanks for your time," she told Frank in a rush, stepping away with her phone pressed to her ear. "Is she on the move?"

"She's getting into her car," Brewer confirmed. "She looks pretty freaked out. More spooked than upset. Want me to wait for you?"

"No. We can't risk losing her. Tail her, and keep me updated on your location." She darted through the maze of blinking machines, realizing she'd be quite a bit behind him once she found her way out. "Don't let her out of your sight, Hawk."

"Hold on. I'll share my location with you."

Her phone pinged with a notification: *Brewer wants to share his location with you.*

"Got it." She slid her finger over ACCEPT. "I'll catch up as soon as I can catch a ride. Keep the transmitter dialed in, and let me know if she says anything or calls anyone before I get there."

"I'm on it," he promised.

It felt like a full hour had passed before she was standing beneath the grand concrete canopy at the casino's entrance. In reality, it had been less than ten minutes. She blinked against the daylight while pulling up the ride-hauling apps on her phone. She was about to open one when she spotted a taxi. Standing on her toes, she waved the driver down. The sparkling clean sedan rolled up to her at a snail's pace.

"How do you do? M' name's Roger," the elderly, silver-haired man said as she slipped into the back. The dark, paper-thin skin around the man's silver eyes creased with a friendly smile. "Where can I take you today, miss?"

Bexley gripped the back of his faded leather seat and leaned in. "Nice to meet you, Roger. I'm Bexley. If you start heading north on highway nine, I'll let you know where to go from there."

His brow lifted. "Sounds urgent."

"You can expect a big tip if you bend the speed limit a little."

Shifting into drive, Roger laughed. "Don't have to twist my arm, Miss Bexley. I used to be a race car driver back in the day."

She decided he wasn't kidding as he skidded out of the parking lot and was on the highway in record time. The kindness in the driver's eyes and his easy-going smile reflected in the rearview mirror while he zoomed down the highway began to loosen the knot in her gut. She took a long, calming breath. Whatever happened next, she wouldn't have to face it alone. Brewer was waiting for her.

Fifteen minutes later, Roger pulled up in front of an older 2-story apartment complex with doors to each unit on the outside. Its address matched the one on Kortney's driver's license.

Bexley spotted the silver rental car, then checked the meter and thumbed an extra $20 bill from her wallet. "You certainly didn't waste any time." She handed Roger the money, grinning. "I'm guessing you won a lot of races back in the day."

"I may've won one or two." The kindly old man grinned back. "Best of luck to you, Miss Bexley."

"Take care of yourself, Roger."

She jumped into the passenger's seat of the rental car, still bouncing with energy as she glanced between Brewer and the building. Relief swept through her with the sounds of someone rifling through kitchen cabinets coming from the transmitter. At least she took her purse inside. "What'd I miss?"

Brewer stretched his arm over the backrest behind her. "She called someone on the way here, told them to come over right away."

"Did she say anything else?"

"That was it. She sounded royally pissed." He tipped his head at the building. "She's the second door from the top left."

A small, decades-old pickup truck pulled into the lot in front of the building. A short, stocky kid in his early 20s with tanned skin and a cleanly shaven head stepped out of the parked vehicle, glancing over both shoulders before strolling toward the outdoor stairway. He wore an oversized gray t-shirt featuring a skull, backwards baseball cap, jeans down around his thighs. Like Kortney, he was covered in piercings and tattoos.

When he knocked on Kortney's apartment door, Bexley gripped the dashboard. "Here we go."

Kortney appeared in the open doorway, still wearing her tunic from the spa. The man leaned in as if to kiss her. Snarling, she grabbed a handful of his shirt and dragged him over the threshold.

*"Get in here, Trip!"* her scratchy voice demanded from the listening device.

*"Good to see you too, baby,"* the man answered with a low, agitated grumble. *"Why won't you show me some lovin'? I've missed you somethin' awful, sweetheart. Three days on the road away from you was three too many."*

Bexley shot Brewer a knowing look before the door slammed shut behind the couple. It didn't surprise her in the slightest to learn Kortney had another man on the side.

*"I didn't invite you here for a booty call, Trip. Some super nosy chick came to see me at the spa today, said she was the captain's daughter. She started asking me all kinds of questions about him…how we met, if I knew he was bankrupt and if I still agreed to marry him after I found out. Then she told me that he died."*

*"How the hell did she find you?"*

*"How should I know?"*

*"What'd you tell her?"* Trip's voice tightened with agitation.

*"I acted dumb, pretended to be shocked about the bankruptcy thing. But…that wasn't the worst of it. Trip, she told me she didn't think his death was an accident. She kept giving me this weird look—I think she suspects I had something to do with it."*

*"Jesus, Kort. I swear to god, if you blow this—"*

*"What's this about a car accident? You told me you had no other choice when he came here that night and threatened you with a gun! You said you burned his remains in the mountains, but his daughter said they buried him! What really happened?"*

Bexley's stomach clenched. She turned to exchange a wide-eyed glance with Brewer.

*"I…ah…might've gone down to see him that morning,"*

Trip told her. *"I called and told 'im your life was in danger unless he came to meet me. He said he didn't have a car. I told him he better find one fast if he didn't want something to happen to you. I cut him off just outside of Papaya Springs…forced him into a median."*

Shock zapped Bexley like a lightning bolt. They were listening to a confession by the man who'd killed her father.

Brewer retrieved his phone from a cupholder. "I'm calling the cops."

Gripping his hand, Bexley shook her head. "Not yet. We need something more than a verbal admission."

*"You what?"* Kortney roared. *"That wasn't the plan, Trip! We weren't going to take him out until after I became his wife! Why did you jeopardize everything?"*

Bexley's throat burned. They'd been conspiring to murder him all along.

*"I'm sorry—I couldn't help it! I just…snapped! He was way too into you, baby! After you told me he'd filed for bankruptcy, I decided it was time to put an end to this! I wasn't going to let another man take what's mine!"*

*"You idiot! Now I won't have any rights to his life insurance policy!"*

*"The bastard was dead broke! You weren't going to get a penny outta him!"*

*"That didn't give you the right to make the decision to kill him! What if someone saw you?"*

*"Chill out, Kort. I swear to you, I took care of it. I bribed the cop on the scene. Terry was an old buddy of my brother's. He made his report sound like it'd been a single car accident. And the clerk at the gas station down the road was too stoned to know his head from a hole in the ground when I stopped to fill up. If anyone started asking around, that kid would never remember me."*

*"Where's your car, Trip? You used it to run him off the road, didn't you. That's why you're driving your uncle's pickup. You're such a moron!"*

*"Would you relax? It's safely hidden in my uncle's shed. I hit the car the old man was driving before it spun out. Some of the paint from it rubbed off on my fender. Once enough time has passed and we're in the clear, I'll take it into the shop to get fixed."* They heard the shuffle of feet, then the wet suction of two mouths smacking together. *"Baby, I swear to you, no one will ever know I was involved in his death."*

*"What do we do about his daughter?"*

*"What about her? If she comes around again, let me know."* There was a weighted pause, then the distinct sound of a gun safety being removed. *"Don't you worry, baby. I'll make sure she gets the message that she doesn't want to stick her nose in your business."*

*"Where'd you get that, Trip? If your parole officer finds out you have a gun—"*

*"You worry too damn much. No one messes with my girl. Not some nosy bitch with daddy issues, and not a dirty old man who was completely worthless."*

Cradling her cramping stomach with one hand, Bexley flung the passenger's side door open with the other. She gagged and cried, but she couldn't purge the feeling of sickness.

"We won't let them get away with this, B," Brewer promised, handing her a napkin. "I'm calling the cops to come arrest these arrogant little shits."

Leaning back on the seat, she patted her mouth. Maybe she would finally be able to properly mourn her father, knowing someone had unfairly ended his life.

---

THEY STAYED IN THE PARKING LOT FOR THE ENTIRE show, watching from the rental car as several sheriff's cars surrounded the building, then led the duo out of Kortney's apartment with their hands cuffed behind their backs. Bexley was numb. The officer Brewer spoke with on the phone was certain they could bring Trip in on an illegal possession of a firearm, and Bexley assumed the way Kortney was kicking and screaming that she was being brought in on obstruction. There would be cause to keep the two in custody long enough to check into Brewer's detailed report saying they'd conspired and committed a murder.

When the sheriff's cars lined up to leave the parking lot, Bexley caught Kortney's angry stare from one of their backseats. Bexley wasn't necessarily afraid of the woman, especially when it seemed probable Kortney would be locked up for a long time, but she could *feel* her seething hatred in that stare.

Brewer turned to Bexley, cupping her chin. "Hey. You okay?"

A tear slipped down her cheek. "I'll get there."

He bent over to kiss her temple. "I think we've seen enough. Officer Parks promised he'd keep us updated on their progress." He started the vehicle, and turned back to her. "Want me to see about catching an earlier flight back?"

Sighing, she thought it over. What she wanted to do most was crawl under the covers with him, and sleep for days, forgetting the rest of the world. What she *needed* to do was enjoy every minute of his company. After all, he'd gotten special permission to stay the night.

"First I need to shower this day off me." She turned to him, forcing the corners of her mouth to lift. "Then I want to take my man out on the town to celebrate."

"You sure?"

She nodded and reached out to take his hand, almost stupidly grateful for the acceptance she saw in his eyes. "This wouldn't have happened without your help."

"You would've found a way." Grinning, he brought her hand up to his mouth and kissed her fingers. "You're the most determined woman I've ever met, B. It's just one of the hundreds of things I love about you."

# CHAPTER NINETEEN

Monday afternoon, Bexley waited at a table for two in a quiet corner of La Belle in downtown Papaya Springs. The Italian restaurant buzzed with professionals on business luncheons, and gal pal dates of the town's elite housewives. Elizabeth waited to be summoned from Bexley's SUV across the street, and Brewer was positioned at a table nearby. He'd insisted on acting as a second set of eyes in case the lovers' reunion went south. As they were dealing with the daughter of a mob boss, Bexley agreed it was a practical move.

While waiting on Barnett Freeberg to join her, she observed with amusement as a young, platinum blonde server with a curvy waist and blindingly white teeth repeatedly stopped by Brewer's table, twirling her loose curls and giggling at everything he said. He threw Bexley comical looks of desperation like he was in actual pain. But any jealousy she'd harbored had vanished that rainy morning Brewer had confessed his love, so she laughed.

Saturday evening in Oregon had been both therapeutic and memorable. They had visited the small town below the casino, and lazily dined at a cozy little mom and pop restaurant before taking a stroll through the quaint downtown. They stopped to admire a charming little bed and breakfast in a stately Victorian house, and were greeted by the elderly owners returning from a walk with their golden retriever. Bexley and Brewer were equally enamored by the husband and wife who had been married for fifty years, and decided to spend the night in one of their open rooms. After Brewer retrieved their bags from the casino's hotel, they snuggled in front of the fire on the couch at the foot of their bed.

It was there Bexley was finally able to process the sinister details of her father's murder, shedding more tears than she knew the human body was capable of producing. She'd been grateful when Brewer didn't say anything, only holding her as she cried. She was only able to pull it together when the owners' beautiful dog nudged its way into their room and manically licked her face until both Bexley and Brewer were rolling with laughter.

The bed and breakfast owners eventually retrieved their dog, and Bexley took a hot bath in the old-fashioned tub. She emerged from the bathroom to find the bedroom filled with lit candles, and her handsome man smirking at her from the bed. The mere memories of what happened next warmed her cheeks.

"Miss Squires?"

A man several inches beyond six feet tall with flawless tanned skin and wavy chocolate-colored hair stood beside Bexley, thick lips set in a frown. He was impeccably dressed in a dark three-piece suit, and made a show of adjusting a cuff to reveal a large gold watch on his wrist. There was no question about it, he was dripping with money. And by the way he flaunted his wealth, he was perfectly matched for Elizabeth.

Bexley stood and gestured to the empty seat. "Thank you for agreeing to meet with me, Mr. Freeberg. Have a seat."

He plopped down into the chair, crossing his arms over his lean chest. "What's this about?" His curt attitude reminded Bexley of a small child being forced to eat their vegetables. "I don't have time to play games."

"Then I'll get right to the point." She sat and rested her forearms on the small round table, leaning in. "I was told you were once involved with Elizabeth Ricci, and you had even expressed an interest in marrying her. Is that correct?"

"That's correct." His lips stiffened. "At least until a conflict of interest arose."

"What if your family hadn't been involved with the Ricci family? Would you still be with Elizabeth now?"

His sky-blue eyes narrowed. "What are you, a relationship therapist?" He half-stood, ready to bolt. "Is this some kind of twisted intervention?"

"It's merely a question."

"Her father was convinced I was dating her as some act of revenge on my uncle's behalf, but I suspect she was the one with the hidden agenda. She lied to me from the start."

"Did you ever stop to consider she may have hidden her family from you because her father had a habit of scaring off any men she brought home? After all, she *did* try to talk you out of meeting him, and she must've appeared genuinely surprised the night she learned you and Mattia knew each other."

His eyes drifted away, filled with pain. "I suppose…"

"Listen closely, Barnett. I'm here because Elizabeth is still in love with you, and she wants to know if there's any chance you'll take her back." She silently berated herself—she really *was* turning into a relationship therapist. Did that mean she could charge Elizabeth extra?

Before Barnett could process what Bexley was saying, Elizabeth materialized, whispering his name with a shaky voice. Her cheeks glistened with tears. "I've missed you."

"Lizzy?" Barnett shot to his feet, gripping her arms. "Baby, what—"

Bexley glanced over at Brewer, ensuring that he was paying attention. Holding her gaze, he answered with a slight nod.

"Everything she said is true," Elizabeth cried. "I only lied to you because every man I was with before you ended with my daddy threatening them with their lives. I pretended to be someone else because I was convinced you'd leave me the minute you found out the despicable things my father was capable of doing. I never in a million years would've imagined that your family had been victim to his business practices." She clutched Barnett's forearms with hiccuping cries. "If you'll take me back, I'll do anything you want! I'll disown my family and run away with you! Whatever it takes!"

Barnett took her in his arms, nuzzling her head. "Oh, Lizzy…"

"Let go of her!" a deep voice boomed behind them.

The restaurant erupted with various levels of gasps and yelps as a silver-haired man with serious muscle gruffly shoved his way through the restaurant. Brewer leaped to action, stepping in the man's path before he reached Bexley's table.

"Just relax," Brewer warned. The two men exchanged a dark look before the older man's shoulders rolled forward, and he took a step back.

Elizabeth marched up to the man. "What are you doing here, Vinnie?"

Vinnie stepped around Brewer, glancing between Elizabeth and Barnett. "Your pops had me tracking this joker after that night you brought him by—wanted me to make sure he didn't set foot anywhere near you again. I saw you come inside, and had to make sure he wasn't hurtin' you."

"I would never *hurt* her," Barnett insisted, taking Elizabeth back into his arms. He suddenly winced. "At least…not *intentionally*."

"My *father* is the only one who hurt someone in all of this!" Elizabeth spat at Vinnie through clenched teeth.

"It's my job *as your father* to protect you," an older man interrupted, seemingly coming out of nowhere. The short, burly man with balding hair didn't share a single physical quality with his daughter aside from their twinned expressions of hatred. "It's not my fault you chose to be with someone who comes from an immoral upbringing."

Elizabeth broke free from Barnett's grip and stood toe-to-toe with her father. "You want to discuss *morals*? That's rich coming from someone having an affair with his best friend's wife!"

Mattia Ricci blanched.

The grunt Vinnie released vibrated down Bexley's spine.

"What'd you say?" he demanded.

Bexley had no doubt both men were toting concealed weapons, and there were dozens of patrons in danger of being caught in whatever blow-out was to come. Her mouth turned bone dry. "Let's take this conversation outside," she suggested, attempting to herd them in the direction of the exit.

Not a single one of them budged.

"I wanna hear you say it again," Vinnie prodded, glaring between Elizabeth and her father. "You talkin' about your pops and Gloria?"

Mattia shook his head. "I assure you, she's only trying to get back at me. She doesn't know what she's talking about." He attempted to pry Elizabeth from Barnett's grip. "It's time for you to leave."

Elizabeth shook her dad's grip off. "I saw the evidence myself, Vinnie! He's been storing keepsakes of their excursions together in that secret room in his office! There's even a video of—!"

"Enough!" her father roared. He lifted a hand to strike his daughter.

Barnett shoved Elizabeth aside, grabbing the old man's wrist before it came down. "You don't get to hurt her anymore, you twisted bastard!"

Vinnie's face was slick with sweat, and he shifted his weight every few seconds. "What's she talkin' about, Mattia? Huh? What video is she talkin' about? Why won't you answer me?"

"They've been going behind your back for years, Vinnie!" Elizabeth cried. "He's not the loyal 'brother' you think he is!"

Vinnie's lips trembled. "Is she tellin' the truth, Mattia? You been sleepin' with my Gloria?"

"Of course not, you fool," Mattia answered, lips

curling with irritation. "Are you going to believe a spoiled brat over your oldest friend?"

Bexley's heart pounded as the two men continued to argue. She had to de-escalate the situation before someone was seriously injured. She rushed over to a set of middle aged women watching the show with equally shocked expressions. "Call nine-one-one. Tell them there's a serious brawl starting up, and there's a gun involved."

Both women gasped, eyes rounded.

"Nod if you understand me!" Bexley ordered.

The women both nodded rapidly. One swiped her cell phone off the table and began dialing.

*"You son of a—"*

With the telltale sounds of a scuffle, Bexley spun around. She saw a flash of metal in Vinnie's hand as Brewer tackled him to the floor. The two men wrestled and threw punches.

A moment later, a gunshot blasted through the restaurant.

People scattered like cockroaches, screaming.

Unable to pull in a breath, Bexley reached for her stun gun and ran for the two men. The frantic beats of her heart were deafening. Brewer managed to knock the gun from Vinnie's hand onto the polished floor beside them, but struggled to break free from the man's grip around his neck.

Bexley pressed the electrodes against the large man's jugular vein and fired. Like a monster in a black and white film, Vinnie fought against the electric discharge, teeth clenched. Bexley panicked. What if she couldn't take him down?

"Bexley! Stop!" Elizabeth shouted. "Let him go!"

Bexley reluctantly backed away. Elizabeth was wielding Vinnie's gun, pointed at her father. Barnett stood watching at her side, utterly helpless. When Brewer rushed over to Bexley, taking on a ready stance, she noticed there was already a dark bruise forming along his jawline.

Hands held out at his sides, Mattia scoffed at his daughter. "You're gonna take his side in this?"

"Why would I protect you when you go out of your way to hurt everyone you love?" Elizabeth answered with a disappointed shake of her head. "How could you do that with Gloria after everything Vinnie has done for you?"

Vinnie rose on wobbling legs, rubbing his neck. "Give me the gun, Liz."

"Why, so you can shoot me yourself?" Mattia sneered.

"If what she says is true, I got nothin' to live for," Vinnie challenged, stepping closer to his old friend. "Without my Gloria, I've got nothin' holdin' me back from spendin' a lifetime behind bars for murder." He motioned to Elizabeth with the wave of his fingers. "Give me that, sweetheart. I'm not letting this go down with you getting even more hurt."

With a little sob, Elizabeth dropped her arms. Vinnie took the gun from her hands and patted her shoulder.

Sirens wailed in the distance. Bexley's fingers tangled with Brewer's. She feared the showdown was far from over.

"You're running out of time," Mattia warned Vinnie. "You really gonna put me down like an old dog?"

"Because of all the other good things you did for me over the years, I'm gonna give you a choice," Vinnie offered, aiming the weapon at his boss's head. "One, I shoot you between the eyes, and call it a day. Or two, you turn yourself into the cops when they get here, and tell them all about the little scheme you've been runnin' on Mayor Hoffman's behalf while he's servin' time."

Bexley's ears perked with the mention of the

man she'd helped put behind bars for drug smuggling—the same man Brewer had unknowingly been working for when he was first out of the service. "What scheme?" she blurted, unable to keep her mouth closed.

Vinnie and Mattia simultaneously glared in her direction.

"Stay outta this, B," Brewer muttered, clutching her fingers.

"What's it gonna be, *brother*?" Vinnie sneered, turning back to Mattia. "I'm not lettin' you walk outta this place a free man after you did me dirty. That kinda betrayal is unforgivable."

Mattia squared his jaw and stood taller. "If those are my only options, then I guess you'll have to kill me. I'm not spending the rest of my life living like a caged animal. Besides, Hoffman wouldn't give me a choice in the matter once he heard I'd ratted him out."

*Ratted him out for what?* Bexley wondered as the sirens grew louder.

"Tell your daughter goodbye," Vinnie prompted.

Bexley saw his finger twitch against the trigger. No matter how much Mattia deserved to die, she couldn't be a witness to a murder without trying to stop it. And if the mobster was committing a crime on the ex-mayor's behalf, he deserved to be locked up too.

She sprung into action. Brewer yelled her name as she collided into Vinnie's solid frame. A shot went off before they slammed into the floor. Bexley's hip stung, but she was sure it was from the impact, and not a bullet.

The restaurant was all at once filled with dozens of uniformed police officers, shouting directions. A set of hands effortlessly lifted Bexley off the floor, and set her back on her feet.

Vinnie's eyes followed her movement with a dazzled expression. "Who the hell *are* you?"

"That's Bexley Squires," Elizabeth answered, smiling through tears. "Best PI in the business."

The hands beneath Bexley's armpits dragged her up against a warm, hard chest. *Brewer.* "You're gonna want to remember her name, buddy, because she just saved you from a lifetime behind bars."

# CHAPTER TWENTY

The gentle lull of ocean waves a football field's length from their backdoor was the first thing Bexley heard the morning Brewer was scheduled to report to the Papaya Springs jail. Sunlight caught the crystal sun catcher hanging in the master bedroom window, covering the white walls with long, brilliant rainbows. The faint odor of paint clung to the tongue and groove ceiling Brewer had installed earlier in the week.

She stretched her arms over her head, sinking a little deeper into the brand new mattress and heavenly soft cotton sheets they'd picked out together. They'd also purchased an antique dresser, a set of couches for the main room, and rustic stools for the kitchen island. The rest of the small house remained empty. Their bedroom was the only area they'd had time to paint, leaving Bexley with something to keep her busy over the next eight months. She was more than ready to accept the challenge.

When she flipped around to face Brewer, her heart skidded to a stop. He was already propped on his side, watching her with a dismal smile. "You have no idea how much I'm going to miss this," he said, his voice still groggy with sleep.

Despite a sudden wave of sadness, she grinned. "You mean my crazy bed hair and dried drool on my face, or getting kicked in the night and having your blankets stolen?"

"All of the above." With a chuckle, he tugged her in closer and brushed his lips over her forehead. "Mostly just you."

Her belly fluttered. She would miss him more than she was prepared to handle, and couldn't stand to talk about it. She arched back to face him. "I almost forgot to tell you—I talked to Elizabeth yesterday. She already moved into Barnett's place in L.A. They're planning a small wedding in Italy next month. They're only inviting friends, which apparently now includes yours truly. She even offered to pay for my flight and accommodations."

"You'd be crazy to turn her down," he told her

with a stern look. "It'd do you good to get out of this town for awhile. You've *definitely* earned a vacation, B. I bet Kiersten would drop everything in a heartbeat to be your travel buddy."

As tempting as Elizabeth's offer had been, Bexley had already turned it down. She wasn't keen on spending that amount of time away from Brewer. Visiting the jail was the only way she'd stay sane during the transition.

"Kiersten is too absorbed in her own wedding plans," she told him. "The other day she spent an entire hour trying to convince me to wear an obnoxiously frilly dress she'd picked out because she thinks her Maid of Honor needs to stand out from the other bridesmaids. I don't know why she's in such a hurry to pick things out when the wedding is almost a whole year away." Rolling her eyes, she rested her chin on his chest and traced a fingertip over the battered flag tattoo on his shoulder, doing her best to commit every last detail to memory. "Besides, I'm starting to think this town would completely fall apart without my services."

Brewer clicked his tongue. "You work too damn hard. When I get out, we're going somewhere to give you a break. No arguing."

"You never told me what's going to happen to

your shop while you're gone," she realized. "Need me to stop in every now and then to crack the ol' whip on your employees? I'm sure I could find some videos on how to rebuild an engine if they needed more hands."

"Appreciate the offer, but Colt Sawyer is going to take over until I get back." With a deep grin, he tugged on his t-shirt that she'd worn every night for weeks. "He's a little more *experienced* in auto mechanics."

"How would you know?" She narrowed her eyes with feigned annoyance. "Have you ever seen me change a tire?"

"No, but I did watch you digging around under the hood of your SUV last week after I told you to check the oil. I'd never seen anyone so confused."

"Clearly you've never seen yourself in the kitchen."

Laughing heartily, he leaned in to kiss her. She clung to him, cherishing every sweep of his lips and gentle brush of his fingertips, wishing there was a way to record the sensation so she could play it over and over while he was gone.

A knock on the front door abruptly ended the tender moment.

"Wait right here," Brewer told her. Grinning

wickedly, he jumped off the bed and dashed from the room with the enthusiasm of a little kid on Christmas morning. Wearing only his underwear.

"You're going to scare away our first guest!" she called out among a giggle.

She pulled herself up to sit in the middle of the bed with her legs crossed, straining to listen as Brewer carried on a hushed conversation with another man. The deep rumble of their voices was interrupted by the deep bark of a large dog. The men laughed.

A beat later, Brewer returned with a young black dog on a blue leash. Its legs were long and spindly, bringing its height up to Brewer's mid-thigh. It had the face of a Labrador and the thick, wavy coat of a retriever. The dog's entire body wiggled in excitement when its big, beautiful brown eyes honed in on Bexley. Brewer released the leash.

"Well hello, beautiful," she greeted the dog, bending down to pet its silky fur. The dog leaned into her hand, stretching its muzzle into the air and wiggling its butt. With a giggle, she quirked a brow at Brewer. "What's this sweet dog doing in our bedroom?"

He shrugged. "With all the enemies you've made, it couldn't hurt to have a backup alarm system. The other one only works if someone tries to break in. Hopefully this guy will give you a little more of a heads up."

Her lips cracked with an immense smile. "He's ours?"

Suddenly *she* felt like a little kid on Christmas morning. Had she even mentioned to him that she'd always wanted a dog, or had he merely noticed the way she interacted with the retriever at the bed and breakfast? He'd already bought the house she wanted. She was going to have to step up her game if she wanted to continue being the girlfriend to a perfect man.

"The shelter gave us a week to get to know him," Brewer explained. "I bought a bag of dog food that should get you well past that. If the two of you get along, you just have to go back to the shelter and sign the paperwork. They'll refund the adoption fees if you change your mind for any reason."

"Your new daddy thought of everything," Bexley told the dog, scratching its neck. "Does this handsome guy have a name?"

"You're not going to believe this, but the shelter named him 'Captain Crunch'." Brewer paused, shifting his weight and grimacing. "They called him 'Captain'."

"Of course they did," she deadpanned.

"Sorry, B. I'm sure he'd answer to a new name."

The dog licked her nose and she laughed. "He'll be a lot of help if I'm attacked by a pint of ice cream." She nudged the dog back, scratching behind his ears. "I suppose we could call him 'Cap'. Besides, not *all* of my memories of the captain were awful."

Brewer watched them with a pleased smile. "You never told me why Danks called last night."

She rolled her eyes. "That's because I was distracted by the hot guy assembling my bed."

"That's funny. The way I remember it, *you* attacked *me*."

"Don't listen to him, Cap," she told the dog. "He thinks all women are incapable of controlling themselves around him." She patted the bed beside her, encouraging Cap to jump up. She rubbed his lean belly, amazed by how much the animal had already eased her anxiety. "Danks wanted to let me know they went through a storage unit Kortney was renting, and came across an addendum to my father's Will. If he hadn't gone bankrupt, Cin and I would've inherited his estate in equal parts…along with *Sadie*."

Brewer's eyes lit with surprise. "He must've really believed she was his daughter."

Bexley grunted. "Yeah well *I* won't believe it without a paternity test."

If she hadn't thought it would upset Cineste, Bexley would've asked the coroner to take a DNA sample before their father was cremated. After the funeral, she researched other ways to prove whether or not Sadie was his, and came across a sibling test. If nothing else, it'd be another project to add to the list while Brewer was gone.

Brewer watch the dog snuggle against Bexley. "Looks like I'll have competition when I return."

"Maybe by then I'll have him trained to attack whenever you try to steal the covers."

Brewer sat down at her side with a weary look. "I can't pretend I'm perfectly okay with leaving you behind," he admitted. "But it's not like I have a choice. So do me a favor and be extra careful... watch your back." He combed his fingers through her hair, stopping to grip the back of her head. "I once lost someone I loved more than anything. I couldn't live through it a second time."

Her breath caught in her throat. "I promise we'll be vigilant," she choked out, nodding.

He gathered her in his arms one last time, and

physically showed her just how much she was loved. She memorized everything about the treasured moments—the sounds of the waves crashing outside the window, the way he smelled and tasted, the gentle slide of his full lips, the tenderness behind his every move, the way he clung to her with regret.

Afterwards, as he headed into the bathroom to shower, tears spilled down Bexley's cheeks. She was equally terrified of losing the person *she* loved. There were far too many things that could go wrong in jail. What if he said or did something to offend one of the other inmates, and they snapped? What if his tendency to be a hero put him in the wrong place at the wrong time? What if Sheriff Blair instructed his cronies to mess with Brewer because of the never ending grudge he held against Bexley?

With every dark thought that filled her head, more tears fell. Whining, Cap quickly lapped her tears with his long tongue. She laughed and wrestled the dog under her arm. He was already proving to be a valuable companion.

She watched intently as Brewer returned with a towel wrapped around his waist, then dropped it to slip into worn jeans and a black t-shirt. *Oh how she'd miss that incredible view.* She was grateful she'd taken a picture of him while shirtless as he ran a roller brush over the bedroom ceiling. "In hindsight, I should've insisted you add a tattoo saying 'Bexley's bitch' to your collection so everyone knows you're taken."

His lips lifted with a grin. "I'll make sure they get the message. Oh, and one more thing." He dug into his jeans pocket and tossed her a set of keys. "As good as you look in my shirt, I have a feeling you'll look even better in my car."

Cap sniffed the black keychain as she inspected it in her hand. "You're telling me that in addition to a dog and a house, you bought *a car*? Never thought I'd see the day Brewer Hawkins became domesticated. What's next? An apron with ruffles?" She studied him with one eyebrow raised. "What about your bike?"

"Still have it. But I always wanted a GTO as a kid. One of my customers brought one in a couple months ago that needed a ton of work. He decided he'd be better off selling it to me than putting in the money to have me fix it." He shoved his hands into his jeans pockets, grinning. "It's parked in front of my shop. Take it for a ride whenever you want. But *please* take good care of it, B. I just finished restoring it last week."

"So no drag racing at stop lights?"

With a deep chuckle, he bent until their lips were lined up. "I wouldn't expect Bexley Squires to back down from a challenge."

They kissed again, not letting up until a car honked from their driveway. She'd made Brewer promise he wouldn't leave her with a tearful good-bye, and had arranged for Alex to drive him to the jail. It spared her the humiliation of possibly breaking down in public.

Brewer backed away, eyes sparkling with humor. "See you tomorrow?"

They'd be allowed visits through the jail's video system three days every week, starting the next day. Although Bexley planned to faithfully attend each and every one, she playfully tapped her chin. "I'll see if I can clear my calendar."

Watching him amble away, throwing her one final grin, Bexley's chest and limbs grew heavy. Spending hundreds of days without him would be brutal. Still, as she settled back against the head-board, she realized that for the very first time in her life, she was content.

The dog barked and nudged the leash in Bexley's direction with his nose. His large, sweet eyes watched her expectantly. Bexley had a sneaking suspicion the dog had also been Brewer's way of making sure she didn't sulk in bed all day once he was gone.

She sat up and ruffled Cap's fur, laughing. "Alright, boy. I suppose I could show you around your new neighborhood."

As she got dressed, she smiled to herself. Who would've thought looking for Cineste would've taken her down such a strangely winding road? Bexley thought of all the adventures she'd had, and tears she'd shed to get to this point. She didn't regret any of them.

# ABOUT THE AUTHOR

With over 40 captivating titles spanning various genres, Quinn Avery honed her talent for crafting intricate puzzles through her smart and quirky Bexley Squires mystery series. Her contemporary suspense thrillers, often set in her beloved locales such as Lake Shetek and Mankato, Minnesota, are nothing short of addictive, leaving readers spellbound with their mind-spinning twists.

For more information, and a free ebook, visit www.QuinnAvery.com.

## ACKNOWLEDGMENTS

A massive THANK YOU to the fans who truly believe in Bexley Squires and this series—especially my beta readers who tell me after each book that it was the best one yet, and immediately want to know when I'll have the next one done! Bexley is hands-down my favorite character I've ever created, and I'm grateful that she's generating a following. Maybe one day she'll get her own television series…

To my parents, Christy Freeberg, Corrie Hanson, Kristie Farnham, Jenny Hanson, Polly Barreto, and Heidi Schutt: your support and enthusiasm over Bexley's adventures means more than I could ever express with words!

Shout-out to Najla Qamber for the kick-ass cover, and Brooke Stindtman for letting me use your gorgeous face to sell books—you two truly rock!

I'm especially grateful for my editor Jodi Henley who worked on this one despite all the "crap" she was dealing with in addition to an epidemic!

This was a hard one to finish among all the fear

and anxiety that came with COVID-19. A special thank you to friends and family who kept me going through all of it with texts and video chats, preventing my mental health from completely deteriorating!

To my husband and two youngest kids: I'm especially thankful to have been quarantined with three (sometimes even four) of the funniest humans I know, because without the laughter I would've only have known darkness during these hard times!

www.ingramcontent.com/pod-product-compliance
Lightning Source LLC
Chambersburg PA
CBHW011415310726
48972CB00011B/2980